YOU DON'T KNOW JACK

A Just Jack Thriller

Also by J. Robert Kennedy

James Acton Thrillers

The Protocol
Brass Monkey
Broken Dove
The Templar's Relic
Flags of Sin
The Arab Fall
The Circle of Eight
The Venice Code
Pompeii's Ghosts
Amazon Burning
The Riddle
Blood Relics
Sins of the Titanic
Saint Peter's Soldiers
The Thirteenth Legion
Raging Sun
Wages of Sin
Wrath of the Gods
The Templar's Revenge
The Nazi's Engineer
Atlantis Lost
The Cylon Curse
The Viking Deception
Keepers of the Lost Ark
The Tomb of Genghis Khan
The Manila Deception
The Fourth Bible
Embassy of the Empire
Armageddon
No Good Deed
The Last Soviet
Lake of Bones
Fatal Reunion
The Resurrection Tablet
The Antarctica Incident
The Ghosts of Paris
No More Secrets

Dylan Kane Thrillers

Rogue Operator
Containment Failure
Cold Warriors
Death to America
Black Widow
The Agenda
Retribution
State Sanctioned
Extraordinary Rendition
Red Eagle
The Messenger
The Defector
The Mole
The Arsenal

Just Jack Thrillers

You Don't Know Jack

Templar Detective Thrillers

The Templar Detective
The Parisian Adulteress
The Sergeant's Secret
The Unholy Exorcist
The Code Breaker
The Black Scourge
The Lost Children
The Satanic Whisper

Kriminalinspektor Wolfgang Vogel Mysteries

The Colonel's Wife
Sins of the Child

Delta Force Unleashed Thrillers

Payback
Infidels
The Lazarus Moment
Kill Chain
Forgotten
The Cuban Incident
Rampage
Inside the Wire
Charlie Foxtrot

Detective Shakespeare Mysteries

Depraved Difference
Tick Tock
The Redeemer

Zander Varga, Vampire Detective

The Turned

YOU DON'T KNOW JACK

A Just Jack Thriller

J. ROBERT KENNEDY

UNDERMILL
PRESS

This is a work of fiction. Names, characters, places, and incidents are products of the author's imagination. Any resemblance to actual persons, living or dead, is entirely coincidental.

ISBN: 9781998005369

First Edition

For the victims of the new Soviet Union, same as the old.

YOU DON'T KNOW JACK

A Just Jack Thriller

"Amicus meus, inimicus inimici mei."

"My friend, the enemy of my enemy."

Ancient Proverb

"The missile is awaiting command,

The Russian Sarmat is ready to strike our enemy.

It's ready to carry out an order,

To turn the enemy into dust.

It has one joy,

To disturb NATO's sleep."

Lyrics from Sarmatushka by Denis Maidanov, elected member of President Vladimir Putin's United Russia Party.

Released by the Russian Defense Ministry on December 17, 2022.

PREFACE

With recent events in Ukraine, the topic of strategic versus tactical nuclear weapons has become a subject of discussion, with the discourse taking a horrifying turn where some believe the use of tactical nuclear weapons is fine.

There is a clear distinction between the two types of weapons. Tactical nuclear weapons typically have smaller yields in the one to 50-kiloton range, and strategic nuclear weapons usually have yields in the 100-kiloton to over one-megaton range.

Tactical nukes are meant for use on the battlefield, whereas strategic are designed to take out large targets including cities.

To put the discussion in perspective, the bomb dropped on Hiroshima that killed 70,000-135,000 people had a yield of approximately 15 kilotons.

Tactical nuclear weapons are serious, barbaric weapons that should only be used for deterrence, not as part of modern conventional warfare. Yet there are those in Russia who are demanding their president use tactical nuclear weapons to turn the tide on the battlefield. The current Russian president has threatened to employ his country's massive nuclear arsenal against its enemies, though most don't believe he would be so foolish.

Yet there are those within the Russian power structure who wouldn't hesitate. The question is, what would happen should one of them decide Russia's humiliation had gone on long enough, and victory must be achieved?

No matter the cost.

Server Room S204, The Kremlin

Moscow, Russia

FSB Agent Teresa Novikov glanced over her shoulder as she rushed to the back of the server room located in the bowels of the Kremlin. She was a double agent, and her handler, a CIA operations officer known only to her as Jack, grunted as he shoved against the lone door, the only thing holding back the armed guards on the other side hellbent on killing them.

A tech, still at his keyboard, turned toward her, his eyes bulging with fear as gunfire continued in the corridor. Her country, their country, was going to hell, and a global thermonuclear war could be only days if not hours away.

Because Jack stood accused of an unspeakable crime, committed on behalf of the American government.

The tech held up some zip-ties. "You can use these."

She grabbed them then pointed to the corner where the man's partner lay unconscious. "Sit."

He did and she bound his hands and feet, doing the same to his friend.

"Remember, if anyone asks, we knocked you out too. You have no idea what happened in here."

He nodded rapidly. "Good luck."

She eyed him. "So, you're on our side now?"

"I'm no fool."

"Let's hope you're not the only one."

Heavy gunfire echoed through the room from the doorway and Teresa spun toward the ear-shattering sound to see Jack with the door open, an AK-74 pumping lead at their enemy, her fellow countrymen, in a last-ditch effort to gain the upper hand.

Against impossible odds.

They had managed to survive longer than they should, but there was no way in hell they were getting out of this room alive.

Sheraton Grand Warsaw Hotel

Warsaw, Poland

Two Days Earlier

"Damn, I'm sexy."

CIA Operations Officer Jack—just Jack, turned to the side, admiring his profile in the mirror. Normally, he was a jeans and t-shirt type of guy—he couldn't stand a suit and tie, but there was something about a tuxedo that just worked. If he had a personal life, he couldn't imagine ever wearing one outside of a wedding, and if it were at a wedding, he certainly wouldn't be the groom. Not with his lifestyle. Working for America's Central Intelligence Agency as an operations officer was probably one of the most dangerous jobs in the world, especially since he was one of their more in-demand personnel.

The powers that be for some reason liked the fact he got the job done.

He didn't mind the danger, in fact, he embraced it. You could get hit by a bus tomorrow or diagnosed with terminal cancer. No one said you were guaranteed to live to 74.5 years just because that's what statistics said the average person lived to. He had already won the lottery by being born in America, where death at childbirth was extremely rare. In other parts of the world, he would have been lucky to see the age of five. He could die tomorrow of natural causes or five years from now in a car crash like his parents had when he was a teenager.

He had grown up in the system, something he wouldn't wish on his worst enemy, though as he thought back on it as an adult, he was part of the problem. He had never given any of his foster parents a chance, lashing out with hate and distrust. He was angry that his parents had died and left him all alone. No aunts, no uncles, no grandparents. There were probably some distant relatives out there, but nobody had stepped forward, and his parents had died without wills. Nobody thinks they're dying in their mid-thirties, so no guardians had been named. As a result, he had bounced from foster home to foster home until he was finally placed under the care of two people who just got him.

Paul and Joanne hadn't treated him with kid gloves. Everyone else had always tiptoed around his problems, his past, afraid to set him off, but they engaged with him, asked him questions, talked about what had happened, about why he was in the system, and rather than make excuses for the mistakes of those supposed to take care of him, they instead expressed not only empathy but the same anger he felt. It had opened up the lines of communication, and for the first time since the accident, he had finally faced what had happened. And with the sympathetic ears now available to him with a lifetime of experience behind them, he learned to forgive his parents for the mistakes they had made, because nobody could be blamed for not planning to die so young.

He had finished his teenage years in the loving home provided by Paul and Joanne and their daughter Jamie, embracing Paul's passion for martial arts. He had gone to college, and when he graduated near the top of his class in International Relations, a passion of Joanne's, he'd been recruited.

And now, a decade later, he stood in front of a mirror in a five-star hotel in downtown Warsaw, preparing to meet with an asset that claimed to have critical information about something going on in Russia. He had no idea what the intel was. She had refused to elaborate, except to say it was critical they meet in person.

He adjusted his bowtie, something Langley had taught him how to tie, his jeans and t-shirt wardrobe providing few opportunities to wear a regular tie, let alone this monstrosity. He left it slightly askew as the fashionistas said it should be, though it had him frowning at his reflection.

Things should be straight.

He fit his comms into his ear canal, tucked in so deep only a doctor would find it. He cleared his throat. "Control, Jackrabbit. Do you read me, over?"

The familiar voice of Control Actual, Chris Leroux for tonight, replied immediately. "Jackrabbit, Control Actual. We read you. What's your status, over?"

"My status is the usual, Control. Damn sexy and ready for action."

Leroux sniggered in Jack's ear. "Is that why you're late checking in? You're having a little sexy time with yourself?"

Jack gave himself a toothy smile in the mirror then grabbed his jacket. "You know me so well. I'm heading out now. ETA at the embassy, fifteen minutes."

"Copy that. Do you have your watch?"

Jack checked his CIA-customized Rolex, far fancier than his usual equally customized Casio, as a coded electric pulse stimulating his wrist indicated Langley's test signal. "Yes, Mom, I've got my watch on. I promise I'll be home by bedtime. Are you like this when Sherrie's going out on an op?"

Leroux laughed at the mention of his girlfriend, Sherrie White, also an operations officer assigned to Eastern Europe. "I'm worse. Just one thing, Jack, remember what happened the last two times you met with this asset?"

Jack headed for the door, smirking at the pornographic memories. "How could I forget?"

"Yeah, well, everyone here in the operations center can't forget either. You left your comms activated all effin' night."

Jack laughed as he gripped the doorknob. "Well, I hope everyone was taking notes because she seemed damn happy with my tradecraft."

"Tradecraft? I don't remember reading that in the manual."

"That's because you haven't read the Operations Officer Intimate Encounters Handbook."

"That actually exists? I thought that was just a rumor."

"That's what they want you to believe. Do you really think the American taxpayer would be happy if they knew there was a lovemaking manual out there for their spies?"

"I think if America knew there was a lovemaking manual out there for their spies, they'd want a copy."

Jack laughed. "You're probably right. When I'm finished with this op, I'll get you a copy. I guarantee you Sherrie's read it." There was a pause, and for a moment Jack wondered if he had gone too far. He had never met Leroux in person though another officer, Dylan Kane, whom he had worked with on multiple occasions and considered a friend, was best friends with Leroux. And with Kane's sense of humor, Leroux had to share at least some of it for them to be so close.

Leroux finally responded. "There's something I should say here in defense of my girlfriend, but since every single word of this is being recorded and transcribed for the record, I'll refrain from commenting until we meet in person someday."

"You do that."

"Enough chitchat. Get your ass to the embassy. The sooner this op is over the better. Whenever an asset demands to meet within twenty-four hours, it always raises red flags and we never get time to set up properly."

"Stop worrying like a mother hen. I'll be fine. I'll be back before you know it."

"Let's hope, and maybe this time come back alone."

"No promises. She's spectacular. I'm pretty sure she's read the manual or at least the Russian equivalent of it."

"You think the Russians have a manual?"

Jack laughed. "Oh, they absolutely have a manual. Trust me. Check your notes from last time. Now enough of this talk about sex. You're making me horny. If all this sexy talk keeps up for the night, I want somebody with a much more sultry voice than yours in my ear."

Leroux laughed. "I think Randy is ready to play Control."

Somebody yelled, "Yeah baby!" in the background, and Jack thanked God it was Leroux's team watching his back tonight. If he was going to die, he'd rather die laughing with someone in his ear who had a sense of humor rather than a straight-laced by-the-book government employee. If somebody new would be in his ear tonight, however, Sonya Tong would be his preference, not Randy Child.

He pulled the door open. "Going silent."

Chopin Boutique Hotel

Warsaw, Poland

Teresa Novikov stood in front of the mirror and stuffed her hand into her bra, grabbing her boob and pulling it up and inward, then repeated the process, turning her respectable Bs into spectacular Bs. Tonight was the biggest night of her career. She worked for the FSB, the Federal Security Service of the Russian Federation, once known as the KGB. What her taskmasters didn't know was that she was a double agent, passing intel on to the Americans for almost three years now.

She should have never joined the FSB, but she had foolishly followed in her father's and grandfather's footsteps. Both had been KGB, and at her father's urging, she had joined. She had always thought it was an honorable profession, protecting one's country. Every major power had its spies, and she had been excited to become one. There was a romanticism that surrounded the profession created by the movies and books, but the reality was much different, especially as a woman. So many of her assignments were the honeypot type, and she had slept with far too many men that it disgusted her at times. But it was all part of the job. Those men were the enemy, someone that had information her country needed, so she did her job and literally grinned and bore it.

Sometimes the assignment was quite enjoyable. Like tonight. She was seeing Jack again. He was an American spy, though he had never admitted that fact to her, not in so many words. They had slept together every time they had met, and she had no doubt they would sleep together again tonight. He was probably the best she had ever had. He had definitely read the manual, and with him, she had the distinct impression he actually enjoyed what he was doing with her specifically, as opposed to just any old warm body underneath him.

There was a connection.

Perhaps in another life, there could have been something there. She laughed aloud. "What other life?"

There weren't a lot of options in today's Russia for people like her who believed in freedom and democracy. Too many like her father and grandfather lamented for the days of the old Soviet Union, and too many of the young who had no recollection of how bad things were under Communist Party rule, had embraced the cult of personality surrounding their strongman leader, and now look where they stood. The pariah of the world, the best and brightest fleeing for economic opportunities in the West, or being sent to war as cannon fodder.

But things could be worse. Much worse. She had come across a piece of intel that she wasn't supposed to see, a misdelivered file, the FSB still liking its paper. As a double agent, the misdirected file was irresistible, and she had opened it. And what she had read had shocked her to her core. She had photographed the pages, returned them to the file, then placed it back on the incompetent mail clerk's cart while he was in another office.

And immediately made arrangements to meet Jack.

As soon as she handed the intel over, she was done. She was out of this game. Not just the double agent business, but the entire spy business. It was too dangerous a life, especially when playing for both sides, and if anyone ever found out that she had seen the file, she could look forward to her final days being dominated by pain and imprisonment.

The question was, did she leave the country? Despite her father and grandfather's long-held political beliefs, and her mother's insistence on ignoring the problems of the world around her and instead keeping her head down and running the household, she loved them and would miss them terribly. Her brothers were officers in the army, thankfully not deployed yet, but she had never got along with them, and frankly could finish her life without ever seeing either of them again, though she wished them no ill will.

She sighed. Perhaps running away wasn't the solution to her problems. Perhaps she should stay and fight to save her country. It was a losing proposition with the current leader, and with those waiting in the wings to replace him, Russia was doomed for another generation. And it wasn't her responsibility to rescue it. What she was doing tonight was enough. It would hopefully provide years more stability, even if it were under the grip of a madman. And perhaps years from now when he died from natural causes, and there could be an orderly transition of power, perhaps then reform could take place.

But if the scenario she had read about were to occur, her country would be plunged into chaos and a civil war that could lead to a full-scale world war.

And she couldn't let that happen.

Embassy of the Russian Federation

Warsaw, Poland

Jack stood with his arms outstretched as a security guard in a black business suit passed a wand over him. He was waved through and he collected his personal items from the tray. He gave each sleeve a gentle tug then followed the guests deeper inside the Russian Embassy. His cover tonight had him as an American Embassy staffer, the Stars and Stripes pin on his chest America's way of flying the flag in the nose of their enemy. The American ambassador wasn't here tonight as he normally would be, not with the current state of affairs, but several low-level embassy staff had been sent as an insult.

Those not schooled in diplomacy might miss the point of the subtle affront, but boycotting an event as banal as this one, put on in honor of the host country, could have one coming off as petty and inflexible. But recall the ambassador for consultations in Washington and send low-level staffers instead, and it turned your enemy's propaganda opportunity into an insult that wouldn't make their state-controlled papers, but the powers that be would know. Wars weren't won by boycotting diplomatic events, they were won through intelligence gathering and boots on the ground.

Jack spotted Teresa Novikov playing wallflower at the far end of the banquet hall. He headed for her, and as they made eye contact, he grabbed two champagne flutes off a waiter's tray. She was as breathtaking as he remembered, though tonight she appeared more nervous than usual.

"I don't believe we've met before. I'm Jack." He held up one of the glasses. "Champagne?"

She smiled. "Thank you. Teresa Novikov." She smirked at him. "Does Jack have a last name?"

She was toying with him. "Of course Jack has a last name." He turned to stand beside her, staring out at the who's who of Warsaw society, far too many of the elite in the former Eastern Bloc forced to play both sides economically. Few Western ambassadors were here, but the Chinese ambassador was, along with most of those from Middle Eastern and African states.

"I see the Indian ambassador is here," observed Teresa.

"I see that. Washington is not going to be happy. When India goes to war with China again, they might regret snubbing their noses at DC."

"Speaking of war with China, here comes their number one ally."

"Who?"

"North Korea."

"Where?"

"At your two o'clock."

Jack turned his head slightly, spotting the diminutive man. "My God! They're all short."

"That's what you get when an entire society grows up with malnutrition. I read somewhere the Dutch are the tallest in the world on average."

Jack agreed. "I read the same thing, and having scaled a few Dutch blondes just to get a kiss, I can confirm it."

Teresa snickered and leaned closer. "I hope you're going to let me scale you tonight."

Jack smiled down at her. "But, Miss Novikov, we've only just met."

"I guess I'm that kind of girl."

"You mean, you're my kind of girl. I suppose you could play Jill to my Jack tonight."

"Really? You went with Jack and Jill? I would've thought you'd have gone with Jack and the bean—"

He laughed, raising a finger. "That would be a little too on the nose, don't you think?" He sipped his champagne. "I wonder how long we have to stay here before we can leave without drawing attention."

"Longer than we have been." Teresa muttered a curse under her breath.

"What's wrong?"

"My boss is heading toward us. Your nine o'clock."

Jack shifted his gaze slightly without turning his head. "Just stay calm. Pretend you're happy to see him, otherwise you risk blowing this whole thing."

She forced a smile and raised a hand, hailing the man. "Director Nikitin, I wasn't expecting to see you here tonight."

Jack turned to see Ilya Nikitin walking toward them. He was familiar with all the senior members of the FSB, especially those in Teresa's chain of command, but everyone was in this man's chain—he was the director of the entire damned thing.

And shouldn't be here.

He downed his champagne as Teresa extended a hand and Nikitin shook it. "I was here on business and was graciously invited by the ambassador."

"Director Nikitin, may I present one of the representatives from the American Embassy, Jack…" She paused. "I'm sorry, I don't think I got your last name."

"Didn't I mention it? I'm sorry." Jack extended a hand. "Jack Palance. Pleasure to meet you, sir."

Nikitin shook Jack's hand. "And what do you do at the embassy, Mr. Palance?"

"I'm just a paper pusher, sir. All very boring, all very routine, I can assure you."

"How long have you been stationed here?"

"A couple of years now. Beautiful city. I love the history here."

"And you're young. I hear the nightlife is good."

Jack shrugged. "Oh, I wouldn't know much about that." He waved a hand at the surroundings. "I think this is the most exciting thing that's happened to me since I arrived in Warsaw."

"Yet the American ambassador isn't here."

"He sends his regrets, but he was recalled to Washington to consult on something."

"It would appear the entire senior staff was recalled, judging by who your government deigned to send tonight for such an important occasion."

Jack shrugged. "Way above my pay grade, sir. Like I said, I just push paper."

Nikitin indicated Teresa. "And how is it that you know Miss Novikov?"

"I don't. I only met her tonight. But when you arrive at a party completely out of your depth and you see a beautiful woman standing alone without a drink in her hand, you remedy that situation. At least that's how I was raised." Jack pressed a hand against his stomach on the right side, just below his ribcage, and grimaced.

"Are you not well, Mr. Palance?"

Jack gently massaged the area with the flattened tips of his fingers. "I'm sure I just did too many push-ups and strained something." He grunted, bending over slightly.

Teresa gently took his arm. "Are you sure you're all right? You seem to be in a lot of pain."

Jack stood upright, arching his back, his hand still pressed against his stomach as he drew a breath. "Yeah, this is no muscle pull. Something's definitely wrong."

"We should get you to a hospital."

"Oh, I'm sure it's not that serious."

Nikitin disagreed. "You should listen to her, Mr. Palance. It could be appendicitis or a gallbladder attack."

Jack groaned. "Or it could just be gas. One good toot and it all goes away. But you're right, I think I'm going to have to leave. I'll just go back to my hotel."

Nikitin's eyes narrowed. "But I thought you lived in Warsaw?"

"I do, but I'm staying at the Sheraton for the weekend. A bit of a staycation to better enjoy being invited to my first foreign embassy event." He groaned again. "I'm done. I was here to show the flag and I'm certain Washington doesn't want it blowing in my own wind."

Teresa gripped his arm. "With your permission, sir, I'll make sure he gets to the hospital."

Nikitin nodded. "Of course, Miss Novikov. Russians help everyone in distress. Even those who would call us their enemy."

Jack doubled over, holding out his empty champagne flute. Teresa took it. "Yeah, I think we've got to go." He forced himself upright and extended a hand. "It was a pleasure meeting you, sir. On behalf of the American government, I'd like to thank you for your hospitality and apologize for making a scene."

Nikitin shook his hand. "It's been my pleasure. I hope you're feeling better soon."

Teresa placed both champagne flutes on the tray of a passing waiter then led him from the room, too many eyes on them for most people's liking, but being seen together in such an obvious manner served his purposes. By making no attempt to hide the fact they had met, and by leaving together, her overseers would be less likely to suspect anything untoward was happening.

It took several minutes for her car to be brought around, and security and staff from the embassy watched on in discomfort at his display. He climbed in the car with the help of one of the security team, and moments later they were off the embassy grounds. Jack leaned over and cocked a cheek, then groaned in relief with a smile, just in case any cameras might catch them.

He grinned at Teresa. "There. All better. Told you."

She glanced over at him. "What do you mean?"

He patted his stomach. "It was just gas."

Leroux's voice filled his ear. "Jackrabbit, Control. The car has been swept. You're clean, over."

"Copy that, Control." He tapped his ear for Teresa's benefit. "My people have confirmed your car is clean. We're free to talk."

"Good to know." She eyed him. "You're all right?"

He laughed. "You do know I was faking it."

She eyed him. "What?"

"The quickest way out of a party is to get thrown out. The second quickest way is to fake a medical emergency."

She growled as she stared at the light traffic in front of them. "You could have at least told me that was your plan."

"If I had, you wouldn't have reacted the way you did." He reached over and squeezed her leg. "I was very touched at how concerned you were for me."

She took his hand. "We have history. Of course I was concerned. But now everyone in that room saw us together."

"Exactly. That's why I requested we meet at the embassy in public after I reviewed your itinerary. You didn't notice anything unusual about it?"

Her jaw slackened slightly. "What do you mean?"

"I mean, you managed to get yourself to Warsaw at the last minute, yet your bosses filled every single minute of it with work, despite the short notice. You don't find that suspicious?"

She shrugged. "Not really. Most of the meetings I arranged myself so I'd have an excuse to be here. What I have for you can't be handed over in Moscow. It's too risky."

"You have it on you?"

"Yes."

"Where?"

She flashed him a toothy smile. "Don't worry, you'll find it."

He laughed. "I can't wait. But back to what I was saying, you should consider immediate extraction."

She pursed her lips. "I was thinking the same thing. When you see the intel, you'll realize that Russia's about to become an extremely dangerous place, especially for anyone who doesn't believe in the old ways."

He regarded her. "Just what is this intel?"

"You wouldn't believe me if I told you. You have to see it with your own eyes."

He frowned. "Something tells me our fun and games for the evening just got canceled."

Operations Center 3, CIA Headquarters

Langley, Virginia

CIA Analyst Supervisor Chris Leroux looked up as the interior door of the state-of-the-art operations center hissed open, the shielded double-doors providing protection against any stray signals escaping or entering the secure room. National Clandestine Service Chief Leif Morrison entered and Leroux rose to greet him. Morrison glanced over at the massive displays arcing across the front of the room, various security cameras and satellite feeds tracking Jack's progress.

Leroux cleared his throat. "Sir, Jack's made contact with our asset inside the embassy, and she's confirmed she has the intel on her. There was an encounter with her superior, Director Nikitin."

Morrison cocked an eyebrow. "Seriously? Nikitin was there?"

"Yes, sir."

Morrison pursed his lips as he joined Leroux in the center of the room, facing the screens. "My last briefing didn't indicate he was going to be in Warsaw."

Leroux agreed. "It can't be a coincidence."

Morrison regarded him. "Do you think they suspect something?"

"Wouldn't you? If one of your officers suddenly demanded assignment to a foreign country with a bunch of make-work projects lined up, wouldn't a red flag be raised for you?"

"It would, which would be why I'd have them shadowed by another officer. I wouldn't personally attend."

"Well, this is Russia, sir, which is no different than the former Soviet Union. They're not known for delegating. It's why they're getting their asses kicked in Ukraine. Nobody in the field has the power to make any decisions. In our structure, our sergeants have more power than their captains."

Morrison rubbed his chin. "When you put it that way, I could see him being there. He doesn't trust anyone else to run the operation, so he's there to micro-manage."

"It's as good a theory as any."

Morrison gestured at the screen. "I take it they've left the embassy?"

"Yes, sir. Jack faked an illness and our asset offered to help get him to the hospital, with Nikitin's blessing. They got in her car and Jack faked a fart on camera. They're heading back to his hotel now."

Morrison rolled his eyes. "God, I hope he remembers to go off comms."

Randy Child, the team's tech wunderkind, snickered as he spun in his chair, staring up at the ceiling. "But that's the best part of the op."

Morrison eyed him. "Son, when you get to be my age, reading transcripts of two young people bumping uglies just reminds you of how old you really are and what you're missing in life."

Sonya Tong, one of the team's senior analysts and Leroux's second-in-command, exchanged a grin with Leroux.

Morrison raised a finger and slowly turned, his eyes taking in the room full of staff. "And if anyone ever repeats that to my wife, I'll set up an Antarctic station."

Laughter rippled through the room and Morrison returned his attention to the screen, reading the AI-generated transcript of what was being said as the conversation played out overhead on the speakers, though at a low volume. "I assume by the way they're talking, her car's been swept?"

"Yes, sir. We have somebody on the catering staff that swept it on a smoke break. No signals were detected. It looks like they didn't expect the two of them to leave together."

Morrison folded his arms and pinched his chin. "Doing the meet at the embassy was a mistake. It's too visible. They should have just done a dead drop."

"She refused. She insisted on doing it in person."

"Which should be a red flag in itself." Morrison sighed. "I just have a bad feeling about this. Jack's cover is solid?"

"Yes, sir, it's the one he's used a lot over the past several years. If anyone takes a deep dive on it, they'll find lots of travel history, a local residence, a car, phones, utility bills, everything. His cover is rock solid. They might have suspicions, but just like us, they wouldn't pick him up for them."

"But just like us, they'd observe him."

"Absolutely."

"Any indication of surveillance?"

"No, but we have to assume there is."

"What precautions has Jack taken?"

Leroux shrugged. "Jack's being Jack, sir."

"What's that supposed to mean?"

"He created a scene in a public place, left with the asset for everyone to see, and now he's taking her back to his hotel room where I believe his intention is to…" Leroux paused and Morrison eyed him.

"His intention is to what?"

"Bang her till the sun comes up," said Child, spinning in his chair.

Morrison grunted. "Well, let's hope he transmits the intel before he does that."

Leroux chuckled. "I've already told him to turn off his comms before they start doing the nasty, but knowing Jack, he'll leave them on just to mess with us."

"Why is it that all my best officers constantly torment me?" Morrison pointed at his hair. "It's because of Jack and Kane that I've gone completely gray."

Leroux eyed the hair, a striking silver that he hoped to have when he grayed. "Well, sir, one positive is that you didn't go bald from it."

"True." He tapped the top of his head. "Though I could be pulling a Ted Danson and you'd never know it."

Child stopped spinning. "Ted who?"

Morrison threw back his head and groaned. "I'm getting too old for this shit." He headed for the door. "Let me know when he's transmitted the intel, and tell whoever's putting together the transcripts for what's about to happen to just leave the AI version for his canoodling. It's less cringeworthy and good for a laugh when it has no idea what to make of what's being said."

Leroux grinned. "I'll see to it, sir."

Danny Packman, one of Leroux's senior analysts, turned in his chair. "He's not wrong about the AI transcripts. They're hilarious. I guess they haven't programmed it yet with the extensive erotica archives that are out there."

Tong snickered. "God help us all if they do. The youth of America will never get anything done."

Child grinned. "To hell with the youth of America, *I'll* never get anything done."

Marc Therrien, a senior analyst and one of the oldest in the room, guffawed. "My God, Randy, if you're not the youth of America then I don't know what the hell is. I've got underwear older than you."

Child rose, facing the team. "Okay, whoever gets him in the Secret Santa draw next year, you know what he needs. New gitch."

The room erupted and Therrien stood, taking a bow before delivering double-fisted birds. "I take a men's medium brief. Black please. Tighty-whities make me feel like a little boy."

Packman snorted. "And they're so unforgiving when you're in a rush with a turtle head."

Tong turned to Packman, puzzled. "Turtle head?"

Leroux squeezed his forehead, closing his eyes. "You don't want to know."

"Look it up on the Urban Dictionary," said Child between fits of laughter.

Leroux cleared his throat and raised his hand, cutting off the frivolity as he pointed at the displays, the satellite tracking showing Jack arriving at the hotel. "Okay, people, eyes wide. We have to assume the exchange will happen as soon as they're in his room." He glanced over his shoulder at Packman. "Confirmed no one went in his room while he was out?"

"Confirmed. The motion detector shows no movement after he left, and the signal sweeper is still showing clear. If they did insert surveillance, it's not transmitting, it's wired."

Passive surveillance was the worst kind. It couldn't be detected and had to be physically found, and searching the room while undercover wasn't an option for it would never occur to an innocent person to search for surveillance.

Teresa brought her car to a halt in front of the hotel, ending the tracking portion of the operation and Leroux gave the order to switch the displays to show the hotel feeds. Half a dozen different images appeared in a grid. "Watch for anybody taking an interest in their arrival. Anybody getting up. Anybody touching their ear, talking into their wrist. Anybody paying attention to the elevator that they get on."

Child pointed. "Camera Three. Guy on the couch reading the paper. He just looked over the top as they came into the lobby then said something."

Leroux turned to Tong. "Check him out."

"I'm on it." Tong hurried to her station and Leroux left the task in her capable hands, returning his attention to the other cameras. The lobby was fairly busy. It was still early in the evening, Jack's faked illness having them returning during the peak of Warsaw's nightlife. Tong cursed then tapped at her keyboard before pointing at the display where a CIA dossier was now shown. "His name is Alexie Orlov. Former Russian FSB, Moscow branch. We have nothing on file indicating who he now works for."

"What's he doing in Warsaw?" asked Child.

"He might have come in with Director Nikitin," suggested Packman. "If he is running an op, he might have brought in all his own people."

Tong dismissed the idea. "It says here he's former."

"Freelance?"

Leroux scratched at his chin. "If that's the case and he's pre-positioned the people at Jack's hotel, then this whole op is already blown." He grabbed his headset and fit it in place. "Jackrabbit, Control. Abort! I say again, abort! We have reason to believe the operation's been compromised, over." He watched Jack board the elevator with Teresa, giving no indication he had heard the warning. Leroux turned to Tong. "Do we still have comms?"

She checked the system then shook her head. "They went dead as soon as he entered the lobby. They must be using some kind of jammer."

Leroux cursed as all the cameras went dead. "Now what?"

Child checked his system. "We've just lost our hack into the hotel cameras. Either we were discovered, or someone has cut off its connection to the outside world."

"Probably the FSB," said Tong.

Leroux pointed at Tong as his operation went to shit. "Contact Warsaw Station. We need someone to physically go in and deliver the warning. It's time to deliver Jack a pizza. Make it Hawaiian."

Sheraton Grand Warsaw Hotel

Warsaw, Poland

Jack pressed the number for his floor then leaned against the rear wall of the empty elevator with two fistfuls of ass as Teresa attacked his neck like a Hoover with a tongue attachment. It was going to be a good night, but he still had a job to do. He needed to upload the intel to Langley before he could enjoy himself. What had him concerned was that he had heard nothing from Control since he arrived at the hotel. Protocol would have been to indicate they had picked him up on camera and to advise him on whether he was being observed.

He released his death grip on Teresa's fantastic keister and she groaned in disappointment. He pressed one of the buttons on his CIA-customized Rolex and the second hand spun rapidly. He released the button, suppressing a curse, his watch indicating it had lost its connection with Langley, meaning his gear was malfunctioning or he was being jammed, though he supposed there was the remote possibility there was a failure with the satellite. The question was, why? If someone was jamming the signal, was it because of him, Teresa, or something unrelated? It would be one hell of a coincidence if it were the latter.

He yawned, pressing a knuckle against his lower lip.

"Am I boring you?" asked Teresa as she released her iron grip on his most favorite asset.

He smiled at her. "No, not at all, but for some reason I'm really tired all of a sudden."

"Well, I'm not, so I'll do all the work." The elevator chimed and the doors opened. They stepped out and headed for his room, and within moments were inside, Teresa tearing at his clothes. He took her by the shoulders and pushed her back.

"Intel first."

She groaned. "Fine." She reached down and removed her high heels, tossing the left one aside, but pulling off the tip of the heel of the right, revealing a USB key.

"Clever."

She shrugged. "We stole it from you."

He chuckled. "Seems like everybody steals from us these days."

"Hasn't it always been that way?"

"Oh, it has, but it just seems it's more successful now than before." He yawned again as he removed his CIA-issued tablet from the room safe. He logged in and the device reported it hadn't been tampered with. He plugged the USB key in, a progress bar indicating the transfer was underway. He tapped the link for the secure messenger but it failed to connect. He cursed. "Check your cellphone."

Teresa pulled it out of her purse then frowned. "No signal."

"They're blocking everything."

"They?"

"Well, it has to be your people, not mine."

Teresa batted a hand at him. "You worry too much. There's no way it's my people. They couldn't possibly know. It's probably the Poles doing something."

"With Director Nikitin in town, it could be any number of foreign intelligence services mucking about."

She dropped to her knees and grabbed his belt, unfastening it as he checked his own phone, his concern growing. He had the intel, but he had no way to transmit it. He yawned again and squeezed his eyes shut. Teresa freed her prize and gushed. "Somebody's happy to see me."

He ignored her and activated a transfer of the file to his watch. He was too tired. Something was wrong. If he didn't know better, he would think he had been drugged. The question was when would it have happened? He closed his eyes as Teresa reminded him why she was one of his favorite assets, but instead of enjoying what was on offer, he was running through the events of the evening.

He had eaten room service. That was definitely an opportunity, however, if his food or drink had been drugged, he should have been feeling the effects sooner, for that had been an hour before he had even left. After leaving the hotel room, he had boarded the elevator then headed through the lobby and outside where the valet had his car waiting. He had tipped the young man a ten Euro note discreetly passed with a handshake. It was a brief physical contact, and anything that could be transferred in such a short amount of time would be extremely potent, meaning whoever was attempting to drug him would have little control over when it would take effect. No, it couldn't have been the valet.

He had arrived at the embassy, let the valet take his vehicle, then passed through security with no physical contact except the wand. Any number of people could have bumped into him at the reception, however, that would have meant a microneedle injection, something he likely would have noticed. He yawned again and Teresa reached up, slapping him on the side of the face. He continued to replay the evening. He had spotted her, grabbed two glasses of champagne, then joined her. It had to be the champagne, but it was from a tray. How could they know which one he would take, because Teresa certainly didn't seem affected, and they couldn't have half the room falling asleep.

He drew a breath and held it before slowly exhaling.

Ignore what they want you to see.

Langley had trained him to observe everything, every detail, no matter how unimportant it might seem at the time. It was a mental trick now second nature to him. He would sweep a room left to right and mentally make note of every single thing and every single one that he saw, what they looked like, what they were doing. He was so accustomed to it now that he didn't even realize he was doing it anymore. He ran through the guests, dismissing them, then smirked. The waiter had come from behind carrying the tray and had turned in front of him only moments after he had made eye contact with Teresa. That's when he had taken the two glasses. He continued forward in his memory. The waiter had bowed slightly then turned around, heading back to where he had come from.

Jack smiled.

"That's better," said Teresa.

There were only two full glasses on the tray. The rest were all empties. At the time, he had paid it no mind, but now it meant everything. They had been waiting for him to arrive, sent out the waiter to intercept him, and like any guest, he had taken a drink, in his case two, since he was playing Don Juan. But why hadn't it affected her? Both glasses would have to have been drugged. His mind was growing fuzzy and Teresa's activities weren't helping him focus. He reached out and tapped at his tablet as he struggled to remember if Teresa had drunk any of the champagne, and if she hadn't, was it simply because she wanted to remain alert, or was it because she knew what was in it? Had this been a setup from the beginning? Had he been betrayed, or were they both victims here?

And as he drifted into unconsciousness, he wondered what the Russian FSB had in store for him when he woke up.

Jack moaned like a Cheshire cat, stretching his opposing paws in opposite directions, relishing the sensation of waking after a good night's sleep. He yawned then opened up his eyes, peering into the near pitch black, the only light from the red LED display of the alarm clock showing 7:55 AM, and a hint of light from around the blackout curtains. He rolled over and reached for the dimly lit light switch panel next to the nightstand. He pressed one of the buttons and a bedside lamp flickered on. He squinted and blinked several times as his eyes adjusted.

He tensed. This wasn't his hotel room. He squeezed his eyes shut and pinched the bridge of his nose as he gave his head a shake, immediately regretting the action as it pounded in protest. Had he gotten drunk last night? What the hell had happened? He opened his eyes again, beginning a self-assessment. He ran his fingers through his hair, probing his scalp for any signs of a head injury, but found none. He continued down his face, finding no evidence he had been punched. He checked his hands for any indication of a fight, finding no new cuts or bruises, only the old scars from previous altercations. He inspected his forearms and frowned. His left was tender, as if he had blocked a blow. Something had definitely happened. The question was what?

He rose and headed for the mirror, flicking on every light as he went. He found several more bruises, all on his left side, suggesting he had gone up against a right-handed opponent. He completed his assessment and it appeared he had taken half a dozen blows but nothing else, and unless there was something going on internally, he would be fine.

Comms!

"Control, Jackrabbit. Do you read, over?"

Nothing.

He pressed his finger against his left ear, but the pinch of a comms unit inserted deep in his ear canal wasn't there.

"Teresa!"

He spun toward the bed, finding it empty, with no evidence anyone other than him had spent the night. He headed for the bathroom and found it empty. She was definitely not in the room. He relieved himself and downed as many glasses of water as he could stand, his mouth parched. He stared at himself in the bright lights of the bathroom, struggling to piece together the previous evening. He was on an op in Warsaw. He'd gone to the embassy, met up with Teresa, faked an illness, and left with her. They had returned to his hotel, then what had happened?

He smiled slightly at a flash of Teresa between his legs. They had made it into the hotel room…his fists clenched. He had been drugged. The champagne. But what about the intel? What had happened to it? Her shoe. It was in her shoe. The fact he remembered that meant the exchange had happened, but then what? He could picture his tablet. He had sent it to Langley. There was an error message. No, they had been blocking all comms including cellular. It hadn't been successfully transmitted. Then what? He fought hard against the block but couldn't remember anything else.

What the hell had happened to him after he passed out? He was in a different hotel room and the decor suggested it was a different hotel entirely. Teresa was gone. Had she been in on it? If she had drunk the champagne like he had, she should have passed out as well, but based upon what she had done, she didn't seem affected. She could have been in on it or she might simply have not drunk enough. He had downed his drink. That, he remembered.

But she was a secondary concern. Right now, he had to reestablish contact with Langley and figure out what the hell was going on. Obviously, the FSB was on to him and he needed immediate extraction.

He grabbed his toothbrush on instinct then paused. It was *his* toothbrush. His toiletry bag sat there, plain as day, everything laid out as he normally would. It didn't make sense. It suggested he had come to this room himself with his belongings and set things up as he normally would upon arriving at any hotel.

He stepped back into the room, his rapidly clearing mind finally taking note of his suitcase sitting on the rack as he always placed it so it would be out of the reach of bedbugs. His heartbeat picked up its pace and he began opening drawers and doors, searching for anything out of the ordinary. He paused at the room safe.

I wonder.

He entered the four-digit code he always used and his heart sank as the safe unlocked. Nobody knew that code. He had to have programmed it himself. He opened it and pulled out his tablet, flipping open the case. The screen remained black. He pressed the button on the side. Nothing. The battery was dead, which was odd. He always kept his devices fully charged if possible, and there was no way it should be dead after just one night unless it had been in constant use.

He sat on the edge of the bed and checked his watch, cursing at the broken face, the device obviously damaged in the altercation that had left him injured. What would he have done when he woke up? If he had woken up, he would have realized he had been drugged, that the FSB was on to him, and that he hadn't been able to transmit his data. He would leave, find a new secure location, transmit his data, wipe everything, then arrange for extraction. And he wouldn't go back to sleep. Extraction would be coming quickly. If the drugs were still working on him, however, he might have only been able to relocate.

He growled. It was so frustrating. He turned toward the bathroom. There was no way he would have arranged his toiletries the way he had if he were expecting an extraction, and for that matter, why would he have taken his belongings if he were in a hurry to get out? The most he would have taken was his carry-on. And what had happened to Teresa? He obviously didn't bring her with him, nor would he, unless she requested extraction as well. If she weren't in on it, she might have already left after he passed out. If she weren't in on it, she definitely would have requested extraction since her traitorous behavior had obviously been discovered. The fact she wasn't here suggested she had fled on her own or he had intentionally left her behind rather than risk escaping with someone who had betrayed him.

Again, a secondary concern.

He eyed the phone. One phone call and he could establish contact with Langley. He noticed his cellphone sitting on the nightstand exactly where he would normally leave it. He grabbed it and found it was dead as well. Again, something that didn't make sense. He retrieved his carry-on and tossed it on the bed, unzipping the front pouch where he kept his charging cables, and cursed. They were nowhere to be found. It was impossible to believe he had thought to pack everything, including his toothbrush, but not his charging cables. Though perhaps in his drugged state, he might have forgotten them.

Backups!

He stepped over to the suitcase, flipping it open and reaching in for where he kept a spare set in case he was separated from his carry-on. It wasn't there. He stared back at the bed.

What the hell's going on here?

His tablet and phone were both dead and they shouldn't be. His charging cables were missing from both his carry-on and his suitcase, and that should be impossible—he would only take one set out for charging. Even if both devices needed to be charged, his cables had multiple connectors—he would never take out both cables. Could Teresa have taken it to charge her own device? He supposed it was possible, but why would her phone be dead so early into the evening?

None of this made any sense.

A police siren outside, faint and not a threat, had him racing for the window and throwing the curtains open. He gasped, stumbling backward involuntarily at the view, for what lay before him was not Warsaw at all, but instead Moscow's Red Square.

Somebody pounded on the door.

Operations Center 3, CIA Headquarters

Langley, Virginia

Chris Leroux yawned and stretched. It had been a brutal two days since the op had gone bad, and in those two days, the world had gone to shit. America was at DEFCON 4, all leave canceled, and NATO was on high alert. Even the Chinese were reinforcing their northern border. No one knew what was going to happen next in the Russian Federation.

Their president was dead.

Assassinated.

But for the moment, that wasn't his concern. His concern was what the hell had happened to Jack. They had lost all contact with him the moment he had entered the hotel with Teresa, and his gut was telling him it was related to what was happening. A Russian FSB agent claims she has come across intel that's critical, insists on an emergency meeting with Jack, the director of the FSB just so happens to be in Warsaw at the same time attending an event so far down the global social scale, he was probably the highest-ranking Russian to have ever attended, then a decorated CIA officer disappears twenty-four hours before somebody eliminates the Russian leader.

Leroux had participated in war game scenarios involving the Russian president, a problem that had to be eliminated. The question always was, if you assassinated him, who would replace him? Terrifyingly, there were plenty of people in Russia who were even more extreme than he was. His rhetoric of using nukes was generally perceived simply as saber-rattling within the Russian power structure for those who truly believed they should be used, and used liberally. If Russia were to nuke a country like Ukraine to achieve battlefield objectives, nothing would happen militarily. The NATO defense doctrine against the Soviet Union invading Europe had always been that nukes would never be used first unless the Soviets reached the Rhine, and the MAD principle of mutually assured destruction kept both sides' powder dry, long-range strategic missiles left in their silos, each side knowing full-well that if they dared launch on the other's territory, the full-scale response would end life as we knew it.

It was why countries like North Korea having nuclear weapons didn't really terrify him—their super-duper leader would never do anything to risk his life. It was countries like Iran that terrified those who truly understood the state of things. It was run by Twelvers, whose belief system encouraged them to do whatever it took to bring on Armageddon so that the Mahdi might return. If the Iranians got their hands on a nuke, would they even hesitate to use it on Tel Aviv if they believed Israel's response would be to wipe out the country, triggering a global war, bringing on the very destruction they desired?

What had him and everyone up the chain of command all the way to the Oval Office concerned wasn't that some religious nut would take control of Russia and launch their nukes, it was that a leader who wouldn't hesitate to use them tactically on the battlefield would, and the West had no response to that beyond economic sanctions. Russia, backed by nukes, could take Ukraine, Moldova, Belarus, all of the former Soviet republics, unchallenged. No one in the West was going to war for those countries. The question was what would happen if they then took back the Baltic states, which were NATO members, perhaps even Poland or Hungary? NATO's Article 5 stated that an attack on one was an attack on all, and in theory, every NATO member, including America, would be declaring war and sending troops into battle.

But that was an article written when the world had a stomach for war, shortly after World War II, where Hitler might have been stopped if there had been a unified response to his initial actions. But today, well over half a century later, when most of America and the world had no idea what all-out war meant, would NATO stand against the tyrant or would it crumble? No one wanted to find out, but right now, they might not have a choice. The news had broken last night of the assassin gaining entry and murdering the Russian president. Information was sketchy, and the airports and railways were clogged with foreigners desperate to get out before chaos ensued.

The door to the operations center hissed open and Director Morrison entered, dark circles under his eyes. The man appeared as tired as Leroux felt.

"Status."

Leroux rose with a frown, shaking his head. "Not much beyond what you already know. We lost comms the moment he entered the hotel, and from what we can tell, they were jamming everything. Hotel cameras went offline a couple of minutes later, then the hotel evacuated, we assume due to a fire alarm. We're going through the satellite images that we have, but it's nighttime and it's from directly above, so picking out faces is almost impossible. We don't know at the moment if Jack or Teresa evacuated with the hotel guests, or if they were transported out."

"And still no transmission from Jack?"

"None. We know that comms aren't being blocked at the hotel anymore. We even had someone from Warsaw Station go in and check the room. They reported their comms and cellphone were working and that the room was empty and that it had been cleaned by hotel staff. Apparently, Jack checked out over the Internet using the automated process the next morning."

"You mean the one through the hotel TV?"

"Yes."

"So, someone was in the room?"

"Or someone hacked the system."

Morrison pursed his lips, blowing air through them. "And that famous gut of yours is still telling you that this is somehow connected to the Moscow shitshow?"

"It just seems too coincidental, sir."

Sonya Tong's arm shot up. "I've got something."

"What's that?" asked Leroux as everyone faced his second-in-command.

"Remember how you had me put someone from Moscow Station on Teresa's apartment?"

Leroux's eyes widened. "Don't tell me."

"They just reported that someone matching her description just entered the apartment."

"Holy shit!" exclaimed Randy Child, spinning in his chair. "It was a double-cross right from the get-go!"

Morrison shook his head. "It doesn't make sense. If she's out there and comfortable enough to go to her apartment, could Jack be out there but still in hiding? Maybe he's lost his comms, and because he knows the FSB is looking for him, he's laying low until it's safe to make contact?"

"It's been almost two full days, sir, and it's Warsaw. He should be able to at least reach a payphone or buy a burner cell, hell, steal a phone by picking someone's pocket. There's no way he went all this time without making contact."

"Oh, my God," whispered Danny Packman.

"What?"

Packman tapped at his keyboard and jerked his chin toward the main displays. "I've been monitoring Russian news. This just came on all stations."

"What's it say?" asked Child, all the text on the screen in Russian.

Morrison frowned at the text surrounding a photo of Jack taken at the embassy function. "It says that Jack is a suspected American spy, wanted for the murder of the Russian president."

The indicator in the corner of the room buzzed, silencing everyone as the color-coded DEFCON indicator flipped from a green 4 to a yellow 3.

Morrison stepped down to the front of the room and faced the terrified staff. He pointed at the DEFCON indicator. "We are one step closer to war, and we know damn well that Jack did not assassinate the Russian president. But as long as the Russians think he did or can claim he did, without proof to the contrary, we could be going to war. Everyone has five minutes to call their loved ones. Tell them you won't be coming home until this is over. You didn't hear this from me, but you all know what the primary targets are. I'll leave it up to you whether you warn them to leave."

He headed for the door. "I'm going to call my family, then talk with the president, and then I need you all to find Jack, clear his name, or all this"—he waved his arm at their surroundings—"everything humankind has accomplished goes the way of the dinosaurs."

Unknown Hotel

Moscow, Russia

Jack grabbed the chair sitting next to a table wedged into the corner of the room. He hurled it against the window, shattering the glass and the chair. He picked up one of the broken legs and used it to knock out the remaining glass around the edges as someone in the hall gave the order to break down the door. He stepped out onto a narrow ledge. He was four stories up from the looks of it, far too high to jump, but he had to take a chance. He hopped up, spinning in mid-air, dropping past the ledge as the door to his hotel room burst open.

He grabbed on to the strip of concrete and dangled in the frigid air of a Moscow winter, wearing nothing but his birthday suit. Shouts from above left him little time to admonish himself for not getting dressed the moment he realized something was wrong, and he instead went on blind faith, letting go of the ledge and dropping to the next floor, his fingers catching once again, abruptly halting his momentum. His right hand slipped and he grunted as he dangled by four fingers. He swung his legs and waited for the pendulum of his body to carry him back. He reached up and grabbed the ledge with his free hand as someone from above shouted. He glanced up to see a head poking out the window.

"He's down here!" the man shouted to his colleagues.

Jack peered down. He was about twenty feet in the air. He could survive it, but he'd probably break at least an ankle, which meant he wouldn't be getting away.

"Shoot him!" shouted somebody and he cursed then smiled as he spotted one last hope. He swung his feet toward the window, then pushed off the glass, sending him sailing away from the building and slightly to his right. He reached out his hands, praying he hadn't just screwed up, and spotted the red, white, and blue, not of his beloved Stars and Stripes, but of his enemy's flag. He reached out and snagged it, his hands tight as he gripped the fabric. His entire body jerked to a halt for a moment before the cord holding the flag in place snapped and he swung back toward the building, still gripping the tainted colors. The cord caught on a loop in the pole, cutting his arc back toward the building short, thankfully sparing him from slamming into the stone wall. He yanked at the flag and it tore away, sending him dropping onto the awning covering the hotel entrance.

Gunfire broke out overhead, bullets tearing at the shingles, and he dove for the edge, flipping over the side and onto the pavement below. His head swiveled from left to right, quickly taking in his new situation. He was on the ground. The gunfire from overhead had stopped, though the shouts hadn't. The civilians were in a panic, desperately pushing to get inside the hotel to avoid the bullets rather than the naked man and his swinging tallywhacker. A Mercedes GLE SUV Coupe pulled up, its driver stepping out. Jack walked up and snatched the keys out of the woman's hand. "I'll park that for you, ma'am," he said in flawless Russian.

The woman's eyes bulged as her eyes traveled down Jack's flawless form, coming to rest at Mr. Happy. "What?"

Jack tossed the Russian flag on the seat then climbed in, wiggling his cheeks. "Ooh, seat warmers." She continued to stare at him as he closed the door, pressing the button to start the vehicle before putting it in gear and hammering on the gas. The woman finally shouted, regaining her composure, but it was too late.

Gunfire rattled behind him as officers stationed outside for the raid reacted. The rear window took several hits, leaving splintered holes. He jerked the wheel to the right, careening onto Nikol'Skaya Street and merging into traffic. He hit the buttons to activate the adaptive cruise control and the active steering assist features, then triggered the voice control to make a call. And cursed. There was no phone paired, which meant the woman likely had it in her purse.

He had to contact Langley, though his first priority was getting out of sight, and that meant being far less conspicuous than he now was. He was in a stolen car, and reports of that fact would be going out within the next several minutes, so he would have to ditch it soon. But he was also buck-naked. It was winter, and this wasn't a Florida winter, this was a Moscow winter. It was damn cold, and his kibbles 'n bits would be pulling a George Costanza if he weren't careful.

The car chimed at him, warning him to prove he was paying attention. He grabbed the wheel and gave it a slight jerk, the warning sensor clearing. He reached over and opened the glove compartment, emptying its contents. He found a pair of man's gloves, which he placed on the passenger seat. He opened the center console. Cigarettes, a lighter, and some plastic straws, the paper straw nonsense apparently not having reached Russia yet. So far, very little of use. He could keep his hands warm or, if he got himself excited, one hand and his junior officer, which would likely make him even more conspicuous. Running through the streets of Moscow naked was one thing. Running with an erection waving hello with a black leather glove would be a sight to behold.

He checked ahead to make certain he wasn't about to run into a brick wall, then twisted in his seat, smiling. Dry cleaning. Two hangers. He reached back and grabbed them, hauling them forward, giving the steering wheel a slight jerk. His first discovery was a dress. He'd happily wear it if it fit, but the second hanger contained a business suit, and it had him wondering who the woman was and why she was going to a hotel so early in the morning with evening wear. If he had to hazard a guess, she was someone's personal assistant showing up to execute the other related duties of her job description.

Russia. What a country.

There was only a jacket and pants. He would still be barefoot and shirtless but it was better than nothing.

He grabbed the pants off the hanger then dragged them into the foot well. He shoved his left foot in, pulling the pants up with his fingers all the way to his heel, then used his chin to jerk the steering wheel as the warning chime sounded yet again. He repeated the process with his right foot then pulled the pants up as far as he could, then thrust his hips up, his shoulders pressed against the back of the seat as he hiked the pants all the way up. He buttoned then zipped them, finding them a little snug, then dropped back down, feeling slightly more human. He grabbed the jacket and battled his way into it as the car slowed for a red light. He loved adaptive cruise control. He used it whenever he had the opportunity, but it was always exciting driving a car that didn't have it and experiencing that holy shit moment when the car he had in cruise control continued happily at thirty miles per hour toward the rear of the car ahead, stopped at a light.

He spotted flashing lights in his rearview mirror. They were closing in on him. He had to get out of this vehicle immediately. The light turned green and he took back control, swerving in and out of traffic before hanging a right and careening down a side street, a hail of angry horns fading behind him. He gunned it, rapidly closing the distance between him and the car ahead then took another quick left.

He spotted a Globus store ahead, similar to a Walmart back home. Not only would a barefoot man with no shirt draw little attention in a place like this, it would have everything he needed. Too bad he had no money. He entered the underground parking and lost himself in a sea of cars before backing into a spot to hide the bullet holes in the rear window. He stared at his broken watch and cursed again. He entered the coded sequence around the face, sending an SOS in the off chance that it was only the display broken and not the inner workings, but it appeared to have taken one hell of a blow, perhaps during the events that had resulted in all the bruising to the left side of his body.

He thrust his hips off the seat and pulled out the Russian flag. He tore off the red and blue stripes, then took the white and wrapped it around his neck like a scarf, tucking it into the suit jacket, making the fact he wasn't wearing a shirt much less obvious. He stuffed the cigarettes and lighter in his pants pocket then fit the gloves in place before opening the door. He stepped out, his feet cold on the concrete. He tossed the keys on the seat then closed the door.

He spotted a sign for the elevators and headed for them. A man walked toward him, his head buried in his phone, oblivious to the world around him. Jack adjusted his heading slightly and bumped into the man. "Excuse me," he said, continuing on with a freshly picked wallet. He boarded the elevator, finding it thankfully empty, and was pleased to see several thousand rubles stuffed in the billfold. It would be enough for him to get socks, shoes, and a burner phone, but not much else. Now it was time to make himself inconspicuous and call home for help.

He just prayed they knew what the hell was going on, because he certainly didn't.

Operations Center 3, CIA Headquarters

Langley, Virginia

"I've got something," said Child, gesturing toward the displays, a shaky cellphone video appearing.

Leroux squinted. "What the hell am I looking at?"

Child pointed. "Isn't it obvious? It's a large penis with a Jack attached, leapfrogging down the side of a hotel."

Leroux watched, now with context, the video ending as the Mercedes Jack had commandeered swerved out of sight. "When was this posted?"

"Not even ten minutes ago. I got the coordinates from the geotag, but the comment says the St. Regis Hotel."

"Okay, I want everyone on this. Sonya, we need guest lists. Check out the video, see if we can figure out what room he's coming from. Check for external cameras that might have caught anything. Satellites. Monitor all police calls in the area, and see if we can track that Mercedes."

"I'm on it," replied Tong, immediately handing out assignments to the team.

The door to the operations center opened and Morrison rushed in. He pointed at the display while staring at his phone. "Bring up secure file Romeo-Foxtrot-Four-Seven-Four-Two-Stroke-Five-Alpha."

Leroux entered the folder identifier then keyed in his password when prompted. Morrison joined him then turned to the room.

"What you're about to see is extremely classified. Don't discuss it with anyone outside of this room. Until this moment, maybe half a dozen people in the country have seen it, and that includes the president." He turned to Leroux. "Play the video file."

Leroux double-clicked on the file, sending it to the main display. It was security camera footage from an elevated fixed position. Leroux rose as a figure entered the frame, his back to the camera. "What are we looking at?"

"Security footage provided to us via a contact inside the Kremlin. Don't ask me who. It's a political contact, friendly with the administration, not an intelligence asset."

The figure headed off frame then the camera source changed. The man entered the frame again, his back still to the camera. He reached into his pocket and withdrew a gun, firing half a dozen times at a figure sitting behind a desk. The target shook in his chair then slumped to the side before the shooter turned, heading out of frame again, though not before revealing his face.

The entire room gasped.

It was Jack.

"Holy shit!" exclaimed Child, his customary spin forgotten. "Did Jack just assassinate the Russian president on camera?"

Leroux shook his head. "No way."

Morrison regarded him. "You don't think it's him?"

"I think it definitely *looks* like him, but there's no way Jack would do that."

"Well, you're in the minority. Right now, the Russians are claiming we did it, and this is going to be their proof. Our contact says they have DNA evidence to back it up, because, apparently, he got into an altercation with one of the guards just after this as he made his escape. The president's already ordered him disavowed, just in case. We've been ordered not to provide him with any assistance and to devote all of our resources to bringing him in."

Leroux protested. "This is bullshit, sir. There's no way that's Jack. You know about our mask technology. We can make pretty much anybody look like anyone."

"Oh, I'm in your camp, Chris, believe me, but the White House trusts the source."

"Did it ever occur to the White House that the source could either be compromised, or perhaps they're being played just like we are?"

"Well, you and I both know Jack is missing in Warsaw, so we better find him so we can prove he had nothing to do with it."

Leroux shifted uncomfortably, his eyes darting to the floor.

Morrison groaned. "You found him, didn't you?"

"Yes, sir. Just a few minutes ago."

Morrison's shoulders slumped. "Where?"

"Moscow."

Globus Hypermarket

Moscow, Russia

The clerk's eyes bulged as Jack strolled in, barefoot.

"What the hell happened to you?"

Jack rolled his eyes at the teenager. "I'll give you a piece of advice. If you're going to sleep with your girlfriend's sister, make sure you don't get caught."

The pimply face stared back at him in awe as if he were a god for having had sex with one woman, let alone two.

Jack held up the wad of stolen bills. "I need a full set of warm, comfortable clothes and a pair of shoes, and I don't have a lot of money."

The kid grinned. "We've got a sale on if you don't mind looking like a dork."

Jack chuckled. "Anything's better than what I've got going now."

The young clerk agreed then led him deeper into the store, and within minutes, Jack was in a changing room, slipping into a white turtleneck and a pair of blue pants made of some God-awful synthetic material. But at least he had warm socks. A red winter jacket was pushed past the curtain.

"Try this, seventy-five percent off."

Jack grabbed it and shoved his arms through the sleeves and stared at himself in the mirror. Red, white, and blue. He was detecting a theme. He stuffed his feet inside a pair of snow joggers, figuring if he had to splurge in one area, it would be this, since he might need to run in snow. He velcroed them closed then stuffed the wallet, cigarettes, and lighter in his pockets before emerging.

He struck a pose. "What do you think?"

"Very patriotic."

Jack frowned. "You noticed that too, huh?"

The kid lowered his voice. "Best to look patriotic these days, even if you don't feel it."

"I hear you, brother. These are troubled times."

"Yeah, and with what happened yesterday, things are only going to get worse."

Jack eyed him. "What are you talking about?"

The kid's eyes bulged. "You haven't heard?"

"Heard what?"

"The president, he was assassinated last night. They're saying it was by the Americans."

Jack cursed. "You're kidding me."

The kid stared at him. "I can't believe you haven't heard. I thought everybody knew."

Jack shook his head. "When my girlfriend tossed all my clothes off the balcony, she also threw my cellphone. I haven't heard a thing."

The clerk rang in the order and lowered his voice once again. "You'd better hope that whatever job has kept you out of the draft so far is secure, because everything I'm reading on my phone suggests we're about to go to war with everybody."

Jack forked over most of his stolen money. "Where is the nearest cellphone shop?"

The kid handed him his change and a receipt, then pointed to another part of the store. "Down this aisle, then hang a left, walk almost all the way to the far end and you can't miss it. Ask for Rita. Not only does she know what she's doing, she's as hot as hell."

Jack eyed the kid. "Let me guess, you want to bang her like a drummer?"

Another grin.

"Then a piece of advice, kid. If you want to score with the ladies, don't be calling them hot and staring at their tits. Look in their eyes and get to know them by listening."

The kid stared at him blankly for a moment. "That shit works?"

Jack shrugged. "I banged both sisters, didn't I?"

The kid grinned. "You are my god."

Novikov Residence

Moscow, Russia

Teresa pressed her forehead against the shower wall as the hot water washed down her body, doing little to relieve her tension. She had no idea what was going on. Jack had passed out, and when she couldn't revive him, it was obvious he had been drugged, and that could mean only one thing—the FSB was on to them. She had immediately gathered what little she had brought with her, including the memory stick, wiped down every surface she could remember touching, then zipped Jack back up, hiding any evidence of what she had done to him as best she could.

She had left, collected her car, and returned to her hotel, waiting to be picked up. But as each hour passed and no one came, and no phone call beckoned her to report in, she began wondering what was going on. She had assumed they had been targeted, but the fact she had managed to leave Jack's hotel unchallenged and no one had come for her suggested that whatever was going on was targeting only Jack and not her. If they were only after him, perhaps if she played her cards right, she might get away with it.

So she did the only thing she could think of.

At 8:00 AM the next morning, she reported to her scheduled meeting. She was surprised to find the room empty, save Director Nikitin, and it was everything she could do not to faint. He indicated for her to sit at the conference table and she did. He sat at the head of the table, regarding her for an uncomfortably long time, and she struggled not to continually shift in her chair. When he finally spoke, it was abrupt, and it was everything she could do not to flinch.

"Report."

Report on what?

She hadn't been on an op. In fact, she had been there to betray her country. Did they not know that? Was it only Jack who was targeted, not both of them? Her eyes narrowed. "Sir?"

"What happened last night after you left the party?"

"Oh, sorry, sir. I took him in my car to his hotel room. It ended up just being gas."

"If he was fine, then why did you go upstairs with him?"

She shifted. They had been watching. A partial truth was probably the best—if they were watching, then the FSB was likely behind the drugging. "By the time we reached the hotel, he seemed a little groggy. I was concerned, so I helped him up to his hotel room. He then passed out, and I wasn't sure what to do. It was obvious that he had been drugged."

"Obvious?"

She shrugged. "Well, sir, a man typically doesn't pass out at that time of the night after only one glass of champagne. Once I realized that was the likely source, I left so as not to interfere in any operation you may have underway."

"Operation?"

"Well, sir, if he was drugged at the Russian embassy, it had to have been by one of our people, right? If not, then we have a serious security breach."

"Is there something you're not telling me?"

Her heart nearly stopped. She had to assume they had taken Jack, and if they examined him…

Her cheeks flushed. "There is, sir, but it's rather embarrassing. It's of a personal nature."

"Tell me what you have omitted from your report. That's an order."

She stared at her hands, clenching and unclenching in her lap. "We…" She sighed heavily. "Before he passed out, we had a sexual encounter."

"If he was so heavily drugged, how was this possible?"

Her cheeks flushed. "Well, umm, I…shall we say, serviced him, and didn't realize his condition."

Nikitin's breathing picked up slightly and his eyes darted down to her chest then to her lips before returning to boring into her. "Do you make a habit of servicing Americans?"

She shot her eyes wide. "No, sir, of course not. I don't know what came over me. He was just very charming and handsome, and I guess part of me was attracted to him due to his vulnerable state."

"I thought you said you didn't notice."

She rapidly waved her hand. "No, sir, I don't mean his drugged state, I mean the pain he was in when he left the gathering."

"And when you left his hotel room, what did you do?"

"I returned to my hotel, sir."

"And you didn't think to report what had happened?"

"I decided it was best not to. Like I said before, I thought I had somehow inadvertently become involved in one of our operations, and since any communications I might make could potentially be intercepted, I thought it best to simply report to the office the next morning, then make a verbal report about what I had observed."

"So, you were going to report to me?"

"Yes, sir. I mean, no, sir. I would have reported to the station head as I didn't expect you—"

"If you were going to do that, why did you come to your scheduled meeting?"

"I didn't want anything to appear out of the ordinary." She took a chance. If she was being played and Nikitin knew she was a traitor, it wouldn't matter. But if she were getting away with it, her question would be expected if she were innocent. "Sir, if I may ask, was it an FSB operation?"

Nikitin regarded her for a moment. "No."

A chill ran down her spine. "If it wasn't us, who was it?"

"We intercepted communications that suggested there might be an attempt on the president's life through American assets based in Warsaw.

When this Jack Palance made contact with you, an FSB asset, he was put under surveillance. We intended to bring him in for interrogation."

"Intended?"

"By the time we got into the hotel room, he was gone."

Her jaw dropped. "Gone! That's impossible. He was out cold when I left him."

"Perhaps he was faking it."

She didn't know what to believe. Why would he fake it unless it was his way of getting rid of her. None of it made sense. "I suppose that's possible, sir, though I swear if he was faking, he did a remarkably good job at it. So, what does this mean? Do you suspect that he's involved in this assassination attempt?"

Nikitin shook his head. "We don't know who he is. A Jack Palance wasn't on the guest list. All we know is he is a low-level embassy staffer, based on our conversation. We had hoped by interrogating him, we could find out if anything out of the ordinary was going on at the American Embassy that could then lead us to who to interrogate next, or perhaps to the assassin himself."

"But if he was faking it, does that mean he is the assassin?"

"I doubt it, but he may have been forewarned. The fact he disappeared, that he faked being drugged with you, suggests to me that the Americans are absolutely up to something, and they've warned all their people to be extremely careful."

She had been dismissed, ordered to return to Moscow where she had been debriefed yet again, this time the interrogation far more intense, but it had given her almost half a day to prepare her answers, and she had managed to make it through the second round before being released.

And now she was just confused, word of the president's assassination last night not shared with her. She had to discover it by listening to the radio on the drive home. Nothing made sense. She was certain Jack was a CIA operations officer, a spy capable of the assassination, but she couldn't believe he would do such a thing. Yet why would he fake falling asleep? It made no sense.

A thought occurred to her that had her smiling slightly. Part of her had been hurt that he would fake being drugged to get out of a night of sex with her, but what was more likely was that he wanted to review the intel. If that were the case, the moment he read it, he would have left the hotel to report to his handlers, since all communications were being jammed.

But the thought of the intel had her even more confused. The president was dead. Exactly as the intel had warned could happen.

The only problem was Jack's side was indeed supposed to have done it.

Globus Hypermarket

Moscow, Russia

Jack activated the phone and dialed his access number. It was answered after one ring.

"This is the operator. How may I direct your call?"

"This is Jackrabbit, access code X-ray-Foxtrot-One-Four-Two-Six-Six-One. I'm declaring a Code Red."

"Jackrabbit has been disavowed. Your access has been revoked. You are to turn yourself in to the nearest Agency facility pending charges. No further communication will be permitted." The line went dead and the pit in his stomach was as hollow as it had ever felt.

Memories of the night he had been told about his parents' death rushed back, the sense of abandonment almost overwhelming. And somehow this was worse. His family was intentionally cutting him off, cutting him out. The question was why, but that was a question he didn't have time to answer. He had to save his own ass, and that meant none of the usual CIA contacts or safe houses were available to him, because not only were the Russians after him, so was his own country.

This was bullshit. What the hell had happened to him? It had to be related to the assassination of the Russian president. It was simply too coincidental. But how was it related? He growled in frustration, the utterance echoing through the stairwell he had secreted himself in for what was supposed to be the call to initiate his extraction.

He had to know what was going on, yet the truth remained, he had no time for that. He was alone in Russia with loud, tacky clothes, a cheap cellphone, a cigarette lighter, cigarettes, and nothing else beyond a few rubles in a man's stolen wallet. He needed help.

Any other day, he would have been confident he could get to safety, but security in Moscow would be incredibly tight if the president had been assassinated. He needed to get off the streets, some place safe where he could think. He had dozens of contacts within the city, most of them Agency-related, but he did have a good number that were his own.

A thought occurred to him. He needed a place to hide outside of the Agency's usual haunts. About a year ago, he had been called into Moscow to aid in the exfiltration of two archaeology professors. He had paired up with an old Cold Warrior named Viktor Zorkin, former KGB, now a member of the fabled Grey Network, made up of retired intelligence operatives from around the world. Zorkin had taken him to a safe house, one that had nothing to do with the Agency. If he could get there, it might be exactly what he needed. Now the question was, how to get there without being seen.

Footfalls below from the parking garage had a smile creeping up his face.

Moscow Marriott Royal Aurora Hotel

Moscow, Russia

CIA Operations Officer Sherrie White wiped the steam off the mirror in a circular motion. She continued blow-drying her long blond hair and opened the door to the bathroom to let some of the steam from the shower out, the overhead fan failing to do its job. Then again, she had put it through its paces with the long hot shower she had taken.

When Jack had been reported missing, she was sent to Warsaw to begin the search after it became evident something was severely amiss. That mission had been abandoned the moment word had been received that the Russian president had been assassinated. Langley had redirected her to Moscow before things locked down entirely. They wanted officers in the country that could monitor things or take action if necessary, and with the increased security no doubt now fully in place, she was quite certain she would be stuck in enemy territory for some time, no matter how good her cover was.

She finished blow-drying her hair then brushed it out, tying it all back in a simple ponytail. She finished her morning ablutions, then headed into the bedroom, glancing over at the TV playing in the background. Her jaw dropped and her eyes bulged at Jack's photo. She somersaulted over the bed, grabbing the remote control off the nightstand, and increased the volume as her Rolex sent an electrical pulse into her wrist, indicating a priority message from Langley.

She fetched her cellphone and logged in as she continued to listen to the broadcast indicating that a man believed to be named Jack Palance, an American embassy worker, was wanted for assassinating the Russian president. She chuckled.

The real Jack Palance must be rolling in his grave right now.

Jack had an aversion to his own last name. Why that was, she had no idea, but he was in the habit of adopting the surnames of famous Jacks whenever the situation required it. What was curious was that Palance was not one of his covers. She had been briefed on them all when she had been sent to find him. This was one of his impromptu creations. It would have been used on the fly, likely verbally, probably on a lark. So, how would they have gotten the name? It couldn't have been from any records search or passport scan.

She dialed Control, and the love of her life Chris Leroux answered. Her heart fluttered at his voice. She had no idea why she was so attracted to him. Beyond the CIA, they had nothing in common. He was an introvert, she was an extrovert, and if she hadn't been sent in as the bait in a honeypot trap, they never would have met. And even if they had, she wouldn't have paid him any mind. He just wasn't her type.

But boy, had she been wrong.

"I was beginning to worry. We've been trying to reach you for over ten minutes."

"I was in the shower. I just put my watch back on. Have you seen the Russian news?"

"That's why I've been trying to reach you."

"Before we get into it, does the name Jack Palance mean anything to you?"

Leroux chuckled. "Besides being the old dude from City Slickers who at seventy was in better shape than I am, he's also the name that Jack gave at the embassy to Director Nikitin. Why?"

"Because that's the name they're giving on Russian TV."

"Yeah, I saw that."

"Well, don't you think that's odd?"

"In what way?"

"If he used that name at the embassy, then only two people ever heard it. Teresa and Nikitin. We both know Jack's not the assassin and that he's being framed, but if he is, why would they use that alias? Why wouldn't they use one of his cover names?"

There was a pause as her brilliant boyfriend worked on the train of thought she had begun. "Wait a minute, are you saying that he wasn't framed?"

She perched on the edge of the bed, staring at the television. "I don't know what I'm saying. I guess what I'm saying is, if they were framing him, they would use a name that they could tie back to him. Using Jack Palance actually makes them look like fools. But if you're not framing him, and you really do believe he is guilty, then you use the only name you know. And we both know Nikitin would be heavily involved in any investigation. As soon as he saw that video, he would've recognized him from the embassy."

Leroux cursed. "I hate that it makes so much sense, but if you're right, then that means Jack could be the assassin."

"He could be, though there's another possibility."

"What's that?"

"He's being framed, but Nikitin isn't in on it."

Leroux said nothing and she could imagine her boyfriend deep in thought. "It's an interesting idea, but then why was he in Warsaw?"

"Maybe he caught wind of something, or maybe he was there because of the meet between Jack and Teresa. Remember, we have no idea what that intel she had dealt with. It might have nothing to do with what's going on."

"That would be one hell of a coincidence."

"Agreed. We need more info."

"You're absolutely right, and I have an idea of how we can get some, but it could be risky."

She grinned. "Count me in."

Grey Network Safe House

Moscow, Russia

Jack jimmied the lock using a credit card from the stolen wallet, then stepped inside one of the Grey Network's safe houses. He doubted it was used anymore, considering the last time he was here the police had busted down the door and arrested him and Zorkin. It was also where he had one of the worst pizzas he had ever tasted. Russians didn't know how to make good pizza. It seemed to be something perfected in America. He had tried pizzas all over the world and some were not too bad, but some were god-awful. He remembered ordering a pizza in Germany with the works. The damn thing came with peas and carrots on it. Who the hell puts peas and carrots on an effin' pizza? He liked pretty much any type of meat on his pizza. Green peppers and mushrooms were fine. He even enjoyed a good vegetarian pizza from time to time, but vegetarian pizza didn't mean every freaking vegetable available at the farm.

Peas and carrots? Ridiculous.

He had never ordered a pizza with the works since. It just wasn't worth the risk. The pizza he and Zorkin had been forced to eat the last time he was here was a poor attempt at an American-style pizza. The key was the sauce. Not only did you need just the right amount so you didn't make the crust soggy, you had to have the flavor. Some bland tomato paste was not a pizza sauce, even if it were the right color. A good pizza sauce demanded fresh ingredients. Ripe tomatoes from the morning market and the right seasonings in the right proportions. When done properly, a crust with just sauce and cheese could be divine.

But peas and carrots, no matter how good the sauce was, never worked.

He cleared the apartment, not surprised to find it empty. There was no evidence anyone had been here in some time, though it had been cleaned after the police had raided them since the pizza box was gone. He turned the television on and switched it to a news channel, turning up the volume loud enough so he could hear it throughout the apartment. He inventoried the bedroom and found some decent clothes, then took a quick shower, taking advantage of the toiletries that were there. All new, all apparently laid out for whoever the next occupant would have been.

He dressed, feeling human again, then checked the kitchen. He wouldn't trust anything in the fridge, but he found some canned and dry goods in the cupboards. He grabbed some Kirieshki crackers and parked himself in front of the television with a bottle of water and the box.

He watched the security footage now playing, leaked to the press officially, he had no doubt, purportedly showing him killing the Russian president. He stared at the grainy footage, wondering why it would be so poor if this took place in the Kremlin. All their security cameras should be upgraded. This wasn't a 7-Eleven that he was knocking over. If he had to hazard a guess, the footage had likely been deliberately downscaled, and there was only one reason to do that, and that was to hide the details. Whoever was on the video appeared to know where every camera was, always keeping his face turned away. That fact alone told him it wasn't him he was watching—he had no clue where the cameras were in the Kremlin. When the figure on the screen turned and looked up, he shivered, a tingle racing up and down his spine, for it definitely was him.

Yet it couldn't be.

Obviously, someone was wearing a mask. He doubted that the Russians would manipulate the image with CGI, superimposing his face on someone else's, as it would be too easy to detect. With a mask, that would be almost impossible.

He leaned back and closed his eyes, struggling to remember anything from the past two days. The radio in the car he had stolen at the Globus had confirmed it was a day later than he had realized, another shocker. He had been drugged at the Russian Embassy in Warsaw and passed out in his hotel room, then he had woken up in Moscow, mid-morning, over thirty-six hours later. What had happened during that time? He obviously hadn't been asleep because he had injuries that suggested he had been in a fight. The report on the news indicated there had been an altercation that had left behind the DNA of the killer. The actual killing was barely in frame, and the footage was grainy enough that when zoomed in on, everything was merely a pixelated blur. Yet the press was reporting the Russian president was dead. There was no way he could see the Russian government allowing that to be reported if it weren't true. He had to accept the fact the man was dead, and he stood accused of killing him.

He squeezed his eyes shut tighter. What the hell happened? Someone had drugged him in Warsaw. He assumed that it was the Russians. Even if he had been roofied and hours of his memory had been lost, someone in that condition could never pull off an assassination. You'd be too groggy and barely lucid. He steadied his breathing, calming himself as he reached into the recesses of his mind, struggling for anything, then gasped as a memory emerged. He was in the halls of the Kremlin, walking briskly. Four guards in uniform accompanied him, but he wasn't a prisoner. They went through a door, two remaining outside. One of the guards looked at him. "Good luck, Jack." The accent was thick. A Russian Makarov pistol was pressed into his palm. "End of the hall, through the door, but hurry."

He headed for the far end of the hallway. He reached out and opened the door, pulling it toward him. He stepped inside. The Russian president was at the opposite end of the room, sitting behind an ornate desk that any tsar would have felt at home behind. The man looked up and Jack raised his weapon, firing six times, all shots true, tightly clustered, where the despot's heart would be. Blood spread as the man collapsed forward. An alarm sounded, the weapon not suppressed. He turned and left the room. A door opened to his left and a guard emerged. Jack spun toward him but before he could shoot, the man grabbed at his arm and landed a blow on Jack's rib cage. Jack flinched, his eyes shooting wide as he leaped to his feet.

"Holy shit, what the hell just happened?"

He muted the television so he could think, pacing back and forth in front of the window, the curtains closed, shutting out the world beyond. There was no way he had just imagined that—it was too real. He had felt the blow and it matched exactly with one of his sore ribs. He had been there. He was the assassin. Yet why? How? It made no damn sense. While he'd love to slap a bullet between the eyes of the piece of shit that ran this country, he would never do it unless it was a sanctioned kill, and it was against international law to assassinate world leaders, a law generally obeyed, otherwise, everybody would be killing each other left, right, and center. He couldn't imagine how he would be coerced into doing it, yet he had the memory. He had fired the shots. Yet why was it that he couldn't truly remember?

There was something different about the memory. What, he couldn't put his finger on. There was a lack of clarity, but if he had been drugged, he would expect that. He had been drugged before and put through his paces. It was part of his training, and he hated to admit that it did feel something like that. Yet he still couldn't see how he could pull off an assassination of the Russian president while hampered by drugs powerful enough to have affected him in such a way.

Could the Russians have come up with something different, something new? Had they come up with something that would make him highly suggestible, affect his memory, but leave him in full control so he could carry out a mission he wouldn't normally? What the layman referred to as brainwashing was real, but it took time. There was no way he could have been conditioned within thirty-six hours—it was impossible. And it wasn't thirty-six hours. The assassination had taken place last night, twenty-four hours after he had passed out.

Impossible.

But if there were some new drug, then it was possible. And it was terrifying. If such a drug existed, it could mean he did indeed assassinate the Russian president, yet was innocent of the crime.

Like the Russians were going to give a shit about that.

One thing about Russian justice was it was swift when it wanted to be, and rarely admitted it was wrong even when it was blatantly so. If they found him, he would be arrested, tried, and executed before anyone would have time to question why he might have done such a thing. The Russian government would blame his government, claiming the assassination was sanctioned.

He sighed. They must be going ape shit back home. He eyed the burner phone. He had to know what was going on and he had to make those back home aware that if he was a participant, it wasn't willingly.

And there was only one person he could think to phone who might actually take his call.

Thorn Residence

Vienna, Austria

Beverly Thorn removed the kettle from the stove, pouring the hot water into her teacup, her entire body shaking from the pain. She had never recovered from the beating received from the Russians, and while she feared for what the world now faced, she took tremendous pleasure that their leader was dead and that one of her own had done it. There was no way it was a sanctioned kill. It just wasn't done. And there was no real reason to do it, unless Washington had discovered something the man had planned that was so outrageous it had to be stopped. But even if they had, there were other ways to go about doing it. You didn't send one of your own operatives in to be caught on camera. You used a proxy or, better yet, sane elements within the regime who would kill the man for the same reason.

It was why she never worried about the Russians using nukes. If the president ever ordered their use on the battlefield, one of his own in the chain of command would put two bullets in his head. Nukes were a no-go and were never justified, not in today's world. In 1945, absolutely. Millions of lives were saved by the sacrifice of the residents of Hiroshima and Nagasaki, but countless more were saved over the subsequent decades because the weapons had been used and the horrors of such use had been witnessed by the world. If instead, millions upon millions of allied soldiers had fought a conventional war against the Japanese, while they would have eventually won, no lessons would have been learned, and perhaps some future incident, like the Cuban Missile Crisis, could have led to an exchange of far more powerful weapons because no one would have truly understood the coming horrors.

Perhaps that was what was going on here. Perhaps Washington had discovered that the man intended to use nukes and that no one in his chain of command had suitably reacted, so they had been forced to deal with the problem themselves. But if Jack were involved, she should have been informed. She was his handler, and had been since the beginning. He was supposed to be in Warsaw on a simple intelligence exchange with a Russian double agent. But something had gone wrong. He'd gone dark until he showed up on her television screen.

She groaned as she sat in her chair, letting her tea steep beside her. Her phone rang with an encrypted call from Langley. Director Morrison. "It's about damn time," she muttered. She took the call, pressing the phone to her ear. "It's about damn time."

Morrison chuckled. "Nice to hear your voice too."

"There's no time for pleasantries. What have you got my boy into?"

This appeared to catch Morrison off guard. "What's that supposed to mean?"

"I mean, he wouldn't go off and kill the Russian president unless you gave him orders."

"I can assure you we never gave him any such orders. We lost track of him in Warsaw, just like I told you yesterday. Has he made any attempt to contact you?"

"No."

"That's too bad. I was hoping we might hear something so we could figure out what the hell is going on. Jack's a wildcard sometimes, but never this wild. Regardless, your orders are not to communicate with him. He's been disavowed. Merely tell him to turn himself in, preferably to one of our facilities so he can face charges."

"Not much of a choice for him."

"No, but that's the official line. We need to figure out what the hell's going on. If he did do this, then he should be brought up on charges, but if he didn't, we need to know who did."

"I'll ask him his side if he calls me, your orders be damned."

Morrison chuckled. "Good. I'm sending you a number now. He called in to the switchboard earlier and was given the standard line. We traced the number. It's a newly activated cellphone in Moscow."

The phone vibrated and she checked to see there was a message. "I've got it. Do you want to know what I find out or is it all fruit of the poisoned tree?"

"Oh, I want to know, but I have a feeling anything he says won't be enough to convince Washington to let us help him."

"There's nothing you can do?"

"Not officially, but I've sent Sherrie White in. She's someone I trust who will do the right thing rather than the official thing."

Thorn smirked. "With a mentor like Dylan Kane, that doesn't surprise me." She shifted in her chair. "While chatting with you has been a pleasure, I'm hanging up now. I'd rather be talking to my boy."

"I'll try not to take that personally."

She ended the call and dialed the number Morrison had sent her. It rang half a dozen times then went to a generic message in Russian stating the caller wasn't available, and also indicating that there was no voicemail set up.

She sent a text message. "Call me. It's Aunt Bev."

She thought of all her assets as her children, and if it were Kane, she might have identified herself as his mother, but Jack's parents were a touchy subject. He had never recovered psychologically from their deaths, from the troubled childhood he had found himself thrust into. He had ended up with terrific foster parents in the end, but that hadn't been enough to slay the demons. He hated the sound of his surname and refused to respond to it unless it was absolutely necessary, for just hearing it was torture, reminding him of what he had lost and could never regain, no matter how much time passed.

The phone rang a moment later and her shoulders slumped in relief as she took the call.

"Hello?"

"Hi, Aunt Bev. At least someone's still talking to me."

Outside the Novikov Residence

Moscow, Russia

Sherrie White sat in her rental SUV half a block down from the apartment building Teresa called home. According to Langley, satellite footage showed her car entering the parking garage earlier this morning, and every indication was that she was still inside. Her orders were to interrogate her, forcefully if necessary. Langley needed answers, Washington needed answers, but more importantly, America did. Her country was being blamed for the biggest political assassination since Archduke Ferdinand in 1914, and that led to World War I. If this led to World War III, there would be no World War IV, and Jack knew that, which is why she found it impossible to believe he had done what the video showed.

She had no doubt Jack wasn't involved, at least not willingly, but Teresa? She was absolutely involved. They had just found footage of her leaving Jack's hotel then reporting for work the next day as if nothing had happened. And the fact she was here at her apartment, free as a bird, had to mean her taskmasters were happy. Yet that wasn't necessarily true. She might be a pawn in this as well, and they might have let her go to see what she did, which would mean she would be under surveillance.

She activated her comms. "Control, this is Skylark. Report."

"Skylark, Control," replied Leroux. "Looks like our suspicions were right. We've got two drones overhead, one monitoring the front of the building, one the rear. We've got an SUV parked one street over that's been idling the entire time we've been monitoring, a four-man team."

"Any evidence they're about to make a move?"

"Negative. Looks like they're just waiting for instructions. We've got a good angle on them and it looks like they're all staring at tablets. Your best bet is to gain entry through the parking garage. Randy's already hacked their pass control and programmed your phone. Just pull up and tap it and you're in. There are security cameras on the parking levels and in the elevator and lobby, but not on the floors. Try to keep your head down so they don't get a good shot of you."

"Don't worry, I have a fashionable hat. I'm going to make entry now. Skylark, out."

She put the vehicle in gear then headed for the garage entrance. She pulled in and put her window down, tapping her phone against the panel. It beeped and the garage door at the bottom of the ramp rolled up. She pulled in then guided herself to a vacant spot near the elevator entrance, and backed in just in case she had to make a hasty exit. Most of the spots were empty, the occupants of the building at work, and she just prayed she wasn't unlucky enough to have selected a spot of someone just out for some fresh borscht or on a vodka run.

She grabbed her hat off the passenger seat and placed it on her head then climbed out, heading for the elevator as if she owned the building. She boarded and pressed the button for Teresa's floor. The door slowly closed and she found her heart rate picking up slightly with the excitement. She absolutely loved her job. She was an adrenaline junkie, but the only thing she could think of that she'd rather be doing right now was making love to her man. Every time she was on an op, her pent-up sexual desires built into a cauldron of lust that had to be satiated, which is why whenever she returned home, she physically assaulted her boyfriend for hours on end.

But she never heard him complain.

A tingle swept through her body as she pictured what she would do to him when she got home. She frowned. Assuming they weren't at war. Langley had said she might be stuck here for a while if things continued to go south.

The elevator chimed and the doors slid open.

"To your left," said Leroux's voice in her ear, the whispered instructions erotic in her current state of mind. She headed left as instructed, again with purpose, as she was still on camera. "Eleven-oh-eight. It should be coming up on your right."

She pulled out a pad of paper, flipping it open to the page she had prepared in the car while waiting. She knocked on the door and leaned closer. Rustling sounds inside confirmed Teresa was still home. She gave it a five count, then knocked again. The door opened and in flawless

Russian, she said, "I have a delivery for Teresa Novikov." She held up the pad, Teresa's eyes bulging at the message.

I'm a friend of Jack's. Just play along.

The woman hesitated before finally responding. "I'm Teresa Novikov."

"I need you to sign this, but my pen ran out. I'm sorry. Do you have one I can borrow?" Sherrie indicated Teresa go deeper into the apartment.

Teresa nodded. "Of course." She stepped back inside and Sherrie followed, her phone in her hand, scanning for any surveillance devices. "Just give me a moment. I know I've got a pen around here somewhere."

Sherrie continued to scan, finding nothing. She stepped into the bedroom then the bathroom, then reemerged to find Teresa holding a gun in one hand and a pen in the other.

"Who the hell are you?" demanded the woman.

Sherrie flipped the phone around to show the negative scan. "You'll be happy to know your people trust you enough to not be monitoring you too closely."

"They don't surveil us unless we're under investigation."

"Then you must be under investigation."

Teresa's eyes narrowed. "What do you mean?"

"Your building's being monitored by two drones and a four-man team. Somebody at headquarters doesn't trust you."

Teresa cursed. "Or they're waiting for you to arrive."

"Me?"

"You know what I mean. You or someone like you. What the hell was Jack thinking?"

"That's what I'd like to know."

"You mean you don't know?"

"Of course we don't."

"So your government isn't behind this?"

"Of course not. Washington would never sanction a hit on a world leader, especially the Russian president." Sherrie stepped closer. "We need to know what's going on."

"What makes you think I know?"

Sherrie eyed the woman. "I've read your file. I know you're not that naïve. You were the last person to see him before he showed up on the news to know what the hell happened after you arrived at the hotel."

Teresa eyed her. "You mean you've had no contact with him?"

"No. What happened?"

"We arrived at the hotel, went to his room, began to…" Teresa's voice trailed off and Sherrie urged her on with a rolling hand motion.

"Yes. Yes. You started to fool around, then what?"

"He passed out. I think he was drugged."

"By whom?"

Teresa shrugged. "It had to be the champagne at the embassy. It's the only thing I can think of. I barely had a sip of it, but he drained his glass."

"That would make sense. Then what happened?"

Teresa shifted her weight from one foot to the other. "I hid any evidence of what had been happening, then left and returned to my hotel. I figured there had to be an op going on and it was likely one of ours.

The fact they never picked me up makes me think it had nothing to do with me. I went to work the next day, met with my director, then was sent back to Moscow. I was interrogated for several hours. Nothing rough, just intense questioning when it abruptly ended."

"Around what time?"

"From what I can piece together, less than an hour after the assassination of the president. I waited until a couple of hours ago then they let me go. I guess they had more important things to worry about than me."

"Well, the fact they've got you under surveillance would suggest that's not the case."

Teresa frowned. "No, I suppose you're right. They let me go to see what I would do." She headed for the living area and sat, indicating for Sherrie to do the same. She took a seat across from her as Teresa placed her gun on the table, still within reach but no longer a threat. She motioned at the TV, Jack's picture once again shown. "What the hell's going on?"

Sherrie shook her head. "I don't know, but there's no way he killed the Russian president."

"It sure looks like it to me."

"Images can be manipulated and that video's grainy for a reason." Sherrie pulled out her phone and brought up the video sent to her by Langley and played it. "Notice how they keep switching cameras?"

Teresa continued to watch the video playing on the broadcast. "Well, of course, he's walking. They have to switch from camera to camera."

"Yes, but every angle has him from behind so you can't see his face until the final angle where he looks up at the camera. They freeze the image and that's all we see. What if everything in that video was real except for that last two seconds?"

Teresa sighed. "You're right, but again, it looks genuine. Look at the floor. It's the same floor. He's wearing the same clothes. The guy in the rest of the video has the same build. Hell, I swear he even walks like Jack."

Sherrie leaned forward. "Did you give Jack the intel?"

"I did, but everything was jammed, so he wasn't able to upload it."

"Huh, well that explains that. Do you still have it?"

"Hell no. I got rid of it on my way back to my hotel. I was sure they were after me, so there was no way in hell I wanted to have it with me if they did arrest me."

"What was it? What was so important that you had to urgently get it into his hands personally rather than just transmit it?"

Teresa shook her head. "No, I'm out. This has been my wake-up call."

A pit of anger flared in Sherrie's stomach but she controlled it, instead pointing to the window and the world outside. "Those drones, those men, aren't out there because they think you're innocent. Think about it. You were the last one with Jack and then Jack is being accused of murdering the Russian president. What the hell do you think is going to happen? They're obviously following you because they want to see what you do or if anyone contacts you. Even if you just sit here and do nothing, eventually they're going to take you in and then they're going to really interrogate you. Right now, you're a possible source of information for them. As soon as they determine you're not, this little honeymoon you're on is over."

Teresa paled slightly. "I need out. Get me out of the country. Get me to America, new identity and a pension. Nothing extravagant, and I'll tell you everything I know."

Sherrie's comms squawked in her ear, Leroux's voice quickly following. "Skylark, Control. The drone on the north side of the building is repositioning. It looks like it might be moving in for a view through the window."

Sherrie cursed and leaped to her feet, rushing toward the bathroom. "A drone's going to be looking through the window at any moment. Act normal," she warned as she rushed into the bathroom, making certain not to hit the door. "I'm out of sight. Report."

"The drone is outside the main window now. It's holding position. Stand by."

Sherrie waited, her heart pounding as she struggled to control her breathing. She had been in plenty of tense situations before, but she was still fairly new compared to people like Jack or Kane. Experienced officers like that might not even react to something like this, but she couldn't help herself. The thought of being captured by the Russians on any other day was terrifying enough, but with what was going on, any interrogation would be brutal and long-lasting before they would finally put her to death after some sort of show trial.

"It's moving to the bedroom window."

She flinched at her boyfriend's report.

Calm yourself.

She inhaled through the nose then held it before exhaling slowly, employing the tactical breathing techniques taught at the Farm.

"Stand by."

She found herself holding her breath, only making things worse. She closed her eyes, releasing her clenched fists, inhaling and exhaling slowly.

"You're clear," reported Leroux. "The drone's returning to its former position."

The tension released like a wave. "Any reaction from the car?"

"There seems to be an intense discussion going on. Hands are waving. I have a feeling they're getting impatient. My guess is there's an argument going on right now on whether they're wasting their time and they should just bring her in for further interrogation."

"She's requested extraction."

"What's the intel?"

"She refuses to say until we get her out of the country."

Leroux growled. "We don't have time for this shit. We need to know what the hell that intel was and whether it's related to what's going on."

Sherrie stood and headed for the living room. "We're clear," she told Teresa. She tapped her ear. "My people want to know if the intel you wanted to hand over is related to what's going on."

Teresa furtively glanced at the massive floor-to-ceiling window that had no doubt been a selling point when the apartment was first viewed, but was now leaving them exposed. She stood and faced her. "If I tell you, will you get me out?"

Leroux, listening, responded. "Tell her we will."

Sherrie tapped her ear again. "They say they will."

Teresa's shoulders sagged. "Very well then. Yes, it does."

Grey Network Safe House

Moscow, Russia

Jack had stared at the text message with a smile. The number matched who had just called a moment ago. It was his handler, Beverly Thorn, exactly who he was thinking of calling. Even if he were disavowed, she wouldn't abandon him. She would at least hear him out. He dialed her Moscow number, and the call automatically rerouted to wherever she might happen to be in the world. The familiar voice answered him.

"Hello?"

"Hi, Aunt Bev. At least someone's still talking to me."

"Jack, have you been a bad boy?"

He chuckled. "No more than usual, I assure you."

"I don't know about that. I don't recall you ever knocking off a world leader before."

He sighed. "Neither do I, and I'm not sure I remember doing it this time either."

"What do you mean?"

He stared at the television screen now on mute. "I don't know where to begin."

"How about at the beginning? What happened with the op in Warsaw? Langley says after you entered the hotel, they lost contact with you."

"Yeah, somebody drugged me. I think it was the champagne at the embassy. I passed out in my hotel room and then the next thing I remember is waking up at a hotel in Moscow with the police hammering on the door."

"Are you secure?"

"For the moment. I'm at a Grey Network safe house."

"How did you know where that was?"

"An old friend brought me here once. It looks like it's been abandoned. I should be good here for at least a few hours, maybe even the rest of the day, but I don't want to just be holed up here. I want to figure out what the hell's going on."

"Well, you've been accused of assassinating the Russian president. I assume you have access to a television."

"Yeah, I've seen it."

"And is that you?"

"It certainly looks like me."

"Well, we both know you didn't kill the Russian president, so they're obviously trying to frame you."

He hesitated, shifting in his chair. "Well, about that."

There was a pause. "I don't think I like the sound of that."

"Neither do I. I have this memory of actually performing the assassination, and I have injuries that match those memories."

"What are you talking about? If you have memories, then you did it."

He leaned back and closed his eyes, the odd memory replaying. "I don't know. There's just something weird about it. It's like I was there but I wasn't. I can't explain it. It's not some pieced-together thing where my subconscious is creating a false memory based on the video they're showing on the news over and over. It's more real than that. When I picture it, it's not a fuzzy mess like on TV, it's crystal clear, but it just doesn't seem real."

"You said you were drugged. Could that be why?"

He shrugged. "It has to be, doesn't it? I mean, there's no way in hell I would kill the Russian president. Not willingly. Have you heard anything about a new drug that the Russians might have? Something that makes you highly suggestive, affects your memory, but leaves you in full control so that you could actually execute an op like that?"

"No, I haven't heard anything, but I'm going to look into it. So, you think it's possible you might have actually done this?'

Jack sighed. "I don't know, Bev. An hour ago, I would've said no way in hell, but then after that flashback, I just don't know. I mean, how else would I have the memories if I didn't do it? This isn't some Hollywood movie where they can upload something into your brain. There's no way the Russians have that kind of tech. I have to be involved somehow. And if I am…" His voice trailed off. "How bad are things?"

"Bad. The Russians are hopping mad, but there's not a lot coming out of the Kremlin officially. Nobody knows who's in charge. Our forces are at DEFCON Three and NATO is on high alert, even the Chinese are mobilizing. Nobody knows what the hell's going to happen. The Russian president was nuts, but he was predictable. Right now, Washington's denying any involvement. I don't know if you've noticed, but they're reporting your name is Jack Palance."

Jack chuckled. "Yeah, I noticed that. I'm guessing Director Nikitin provided the identity, which is interesting in itself. If he was in Warsaw because of the meet between me and Teresa, I would've thought he'd at least have my cover name, not my just-having-fun-with-you name."

"That is interesting, isn't it? If he wasn't there because of you, then why in the hell was the director of the FSB in Warsaw at some insignificant event? That'd be like the director of the CIA showing up at a cocktail party in Belarus."

"When did he return to Moscow?"

"Not until after the assassination."

Jack chewed his cheek. "Establishing an alibi?"

Thorn remained silent for a moment. "That's a definite possibility, isn't it? I'm going to let you go now. I have to contact Langley with this new information."

"Do you think they'll change their mind about me?"

"I highly doubt it, considering you actually remember killing the man."

Jack frowned. "Maybe I shouldn't have mentioned it."

She laughed. "I don't know if I would have, but the fact you did tells me, if you are involved, it isn't willingly."

"Let's hope they see it that way, too. But in the meantime, I need to plan for the worst. I need everything. Clothes, papers, cash, phones, weapons."

"Text me your location. I'll arrange a drop outside of normal channels."

"Thanks. I knew I could count on you."

"You know I never abandon my people, no matter what Langley orders."

"Thank God for that."

"All right, I'm letting you go now. Expect a supply run within two hours."

"I'm going to destroy my phone, so I'll be incommunicado."

"Negative, not necessary. All Grey Network safe houses have cellular relays. Right now, my system is telling me you're at the Sheraton Hotel near the airport. That's the only reason why I let us have such an open conversation. Even if they're monitoring, they can't trace you."

"You have to love the Grey Network. Good thing they left things up and running."

"Trust me, they had their reasons, I'm sure. I have no doubt they monitored this conversation and are deciding what to do about it."

Jack frowned. "So, I might not have to worry about the Russians, but the Grey Network could be coming for me?"

"They're not who you have to be worried about. They wouldn't blindly believe the official line, nor are they bound by Washington's whims. But just in case, for you old fogies listening in, I'm just as old as you are. If you're not going to help, then leave my boy alone."

Jack grinned. "I'm sure that'll work. Just get those supplies to me ASAP. And if you can locate another safe house, I'd appreciate it."

"I'll find you a location. Just sit tight, talk to you soon."

The call ended and Jack leaned back, closing his eyes, the odd memory replaying yet again. There was definitely something wrong with it, but what it was, he just couldn't put his finger on it. Deep down, he knew he hadn't done this. There was no way. And the fact there was something wrong with the memory, something off about it, only confirmed his belief, which meant he had to look at things differently. There was only one piece of evidence out there in the world, and that was the video, which he was certain had to have been faked in some way. There would be only one way to prove his innocence, and that was to find the real killer.

But how the hell was he going to do that without Langley's help?

Operations Center 3, CIA Headquarters

Langley, Virginia

Leroux stared at the video for the umpteenth time, just as agencies around the world were likely doing. This was probably the most important security footage ever released to the public, and could start a war if he couldn't prove it was fake. It had to be. Jack had reached out to his handler, Beverly Thorn, and explained his side of things. Morrison had sent him her summary of the conversation, and it didn't set his mind at ease.

Morrison had officially informed her not to have any further interactions with her officer, but that was just for the record. There was no way in hell she would follow that order, especially with what Jack had said. He had been drugged then woke up in Moscow thirty-six hours later, yet he had a memory of committing the assassination. There were combinations of drugs that could do what Jack suggested, that could make someone highly suggestible, another that could wipe their short-term memory. The problem was there was no drug that they were aware of that when combined with the others would leave him with his faculties intact so he might successfully pull off the assassination. The fact he claimed to have a memory of doing it simply didn't make sense.

Tong turned her chair to face him, having just read Thorn's report. "This doesn't make sense."

"You're telling me."

"If he remembers doing it, he had to have done it, right?"

Leroux splayed his hands. "I don't see any other explanation."

"So, if we assume he did it, and he wasn't under the influence of drugs while he did it, then the question is, why did he do it?"

Leroux leaned forward. "Go on."

"Well, we have to assume he didn't do it out of malice and that this wasn't his idea."

Child interrupted. "Why do we have to assume that? Pretty much anybody on the planet would put a bullet in that man's head if they had a chance. He's a murdering dictator piece of shit who deserves to die a horrible death."

Leroux turned in his chair to face their tech wunderkind. "While I would agree with the sentiment, the average John or Jane Doe stumbling upon the opportunity and killing the Russian president would be one thing. But even if Jack had the opportunity, he's an employee of the United States government and he would never exercise that opportunity, because he would know it's an act of war. There's no way he would do this on his own volition."

"Exactly what I was saying," agreed Tong, giving Child a brief stink-eye for interrupting her. "So, if we assume that this wasn't his idea, then I can think of only two possibilities."

Leroux cocked an eyebrow. "Two?"

"Yes. One, that he was coerced somehow into doing it. What that coercion could possibly be, I have no idea. Like you said, an American government asset killing the Russian president is an act of war. What they could have possibly used to force him into doing this is beyond me. He would have to know that any lives he might save would be peanuts compared to the potential cost if we go to war."

"Agreed. But you said two possibilities."

Tong nodded. "I did. And now that I think about it, that second possibility can be broken into two. One, is that he was made to believe the orders came from Washington."

Leroux chewed his cheek for a moment as his head slowly bobbed. "That would certainly explain a few things. And the other?"

Tong glanced about then leaned in, lowering her voice. "The orders *did* come from Washington."

The entire room fell silent at the terrifying suggestion. On the surface, it was outrageous, yet they had only recently dealt with a situation that involved Director Morrison himself from the late eighties where KGB and CIA rogue operatives plotted to assassinate Soviet President Gorbachev. Morrison had helped foil the attempt at the beginning of his career. Leroux closed his eyes and pinched the bridge of his nose. There was no way this could be state sanctioned, yet history proved otherwise.

Leroux rose. "Can I have everyone's attention, please?"

Everyone stopped what they were doing.

"That possibility that was just suggested doesn't leave this room. No chit-chats with your other halves, no whispers in the bathroom, no asides in the elevator. Nothing. While I doubt it's true, in fact, I'm sure it's not true, if a rumor like that started to spread, you could be responsible for triggering World War Three. Right now, at least we have the plausible explanation that Jack was rogue if he did do this, which I'm still not convinced of. But if a rumor gets out there that this was sanctioned, all bets are off.

"You know as well as I do that we game these scenarios all the time. There are rooms filled with people that all they do day-in and day-out is play what-if scenarios, and I have no doubt that somewhere someone has played out what would happen if we assassinated the Russian president. And there's probably even a scenario out there that shows the world would be better off with him dead. All we need is this rumor spreading, then for some do-gooder with more heart than brains to leak that actual scenario. We could be looking at all-out war. So, on this one, zip it, and I mean it. If I catch wind that anybody's discussed this outside of this room, they're off the team. And here's another reason to keep your lips shut. If it were true, and they find out you're discussing it, how long do you think it'll be before you find an assassin's bullet in your own head?"

Tong sucked in a quick breath. "And if anyone asks, please don't tell them it was my idea."

"Oh, shit."

Leroux spun toward Danny Packman. "What is it?"

The analyst tapped at his keyboard then pointed at the screen, the audio from a breaking news report from the BBC piping through the overhead speakers.

"*—has just confirmed that Major General Dmitri Kalishnik, known for his brutal campaigns in Chechnya and Syria, and an extreme hardliner who had grown critical of the Russian president due to his failures in Ukraine, has just claimed the presidency. The elected Federal Assembly of Russia hasn't replied officially yet, but the emergency session that was to begin in just one hour has been postponed, with no new start time given. We are already receiving reports of Russian military units pledging their allegiance to the self-declared president, including Colonel General Andropov, the Commander of the Strategic Rocket Forces of the Russian Federation, the branch of the military responsible for their land-based nuclear arsenal. Prime Minister—*"

Leroux indicated for the audio to be cut and Packman tapped a key, killing the sound. Leroux's entire body demanded he tremble with fear, yet he was the leader of this team, and as he turned, the terror was obvious. Some stared at the screen slack-jawed, others with wide eyes, yet others sobbing quietly. This was the worst-case scenario. General Kalishnik had been calling for immediate nuclear engagement, including retaliatory strikes against NATO for interfering in the conflict in Ukraine, directly blaming the tens of thousands of Russian casualties on the Western alliance. If he managed to gain control with the same level of power his predecessor had, there would be no checks and balances like the former Soviet Union had, no Politburo, no inner circle of advisors. Just one warmonger ready, willing, and able to unleash the nuclear arsenal of a bygone era, and bringing the Soviet Union back to life.

A buzzer sounded and he flinched as the DEFCON indicator switched from 3 to 2 for the first time in over thirty years. They were one step away from war, and the end of life as they knew it.

Novikov Residence

Moscow, Russia

Sherrie regarded Teresa with a smirk. "If Jack has a type, I'm now it."

Teresa laughed and faced the mirror, staring at their reflection. "I don't know if he's got a type, but we could definitely be twins."

"Now, you know where all the cameras are?"

"Yes."

"Good. Just make sure they don't get a clear shot of your face." Sherrie gestured at her clothes now worn by the similarly sized Russian. "They should recognize the outfit and they'll definitely recognize the hat."

Teresa grunted. "Don't be so sure about that. They are all men, after all."

"True. Then let's hope their training went a little bit beyond ogling."

Teresa laughed. "This is modern Russia, as sexist as the old. But you're right, they are trained. At a minimum, they should bring up the footage of you arriving and compare it."

"Just keep that hat in place, your head level, and don't do anything memorable." Sherrie handed over the car keys. "It's a white Hyundai Creta SUV, second parking level, spot two-oh-eight." She handed Teresa the phone. "Just tap this to the panel to open the gate."

"Oh, I've got my own pass."

"No, you can't use that. They might be monitoring the system. In fact, leave anything with an RFID behind. We can't risk you getting caught by some automatic scanner."

"My purse is shielded." Teresa fetched it off the counter. "I'll leave my phone here, turned on."

Sherrie held up a finger. "Control, Skylark. I'm giving her my comms, over."

"Understood, Skylark. We'll pick you up at the rendezvous point. Good luck. By the way, we're at DEFCON Two."

Sherrie's chest ached at the news from her boyfriend. DEFCON 2 meant war was imminent, all-out war, not some limited conflict like Afghanistan or Iraq, where America was never really in danger. War with a failed state like Afghanistan could never compare to war with a former superpower armed with nuclear weapons.

Teresa caught her change in mood. "What's wrong?"

Sherrie dismissed the question with a shake of the head. "Acknowledged, Control. Switching comms now, Skylark, out." She reached into her ear and pinched a small tendril disguised as an ear hair, then pulled on it, the tiny device emerging a moment later. She washed it off in the sink then helped Teresa insert it deep into the ear canal.

"What's my code name?"

"Jack's tagged you as Red Sonja."

"Sonja?"

Sherrie rolled her eyes. "I think he has a thing for Brigitte Nielsen. He's into eighties action movies."

Teresa grinned. "Who isn't? Back when men were men, and if they were in touch with their feelings, it meant the guy they were beating up was named Feelings."

Sherrie laughed. "Press on your ear. Let's do a Comms check."

Teresa pressed her finger against the tragus of her ear, creating a pressure change that toggled the device. "Control, this is Red Sonja, do you read, over?" She paused then gave a thumbs-up. "Copy that, Control, I read you. Red Sonja, out." She reached up to deactivate the comms when Sherrie stopped her.

"No. Leave it on until we rendezvous. Only deactivate it if you think you're going to get scanned."

"All right." Teresa adjusted the wide-brimmed hat Sherrie had given her then faced her rescuer. "Are you going to be all right?"

"I'll be fine. Don't you worry. I'll be five minutes behind you, though it'll probably take me longer to rendezvous with you, especially if they pick me up."

Teresa gestured at the colorful winter jacket she had lent her. "They'll definitely recognize that. If they ask where you got it, you bought it on clearance at the Levsha Flea Market last spring. There was a bunch of them on sale."

"Is that the truth?"

"It is."

"Good."

"Always better to go with the truth whenever possible."

"Same thing they teach us at the Farm." Sherrie stepped out of the bathroom and Teresa followed. She gave the woman a hug. "Good luck. We'll see you soon. Trust the voice in your ear. He's never let me down."

Teresa gave a curt nod and headed out the door, leaving Sherrie alone and checking her watch, the CIA-customized Rolex now her only lifeline.

Operations Center 3, CIA Headquarters

Langley, Virginia

"Whatever you do, don't acknowledge anything I say, and don't touch your ear unless I give you a specific instruction. Cough if you understand me."

Teresa coughed as instructed and Leroux could tell from her body language on the elevator camera feed that she was tense.

"Take a deep breath and slowly let it out. You have to relax. Everything's going to be all right." He muted his mic. "Any evidence they're reacting?"

"Negative," replied Tong. "Drones haven't moved and their team is still just sitting there."

He reactivated his comms. "There's no reaction from the drones or the surveillance team. Right now, they have no idea that it's you. So just relax. You're going to be all right. Just remember to breathe."

The elevator doors opened and a man stepped on. An involuntary gasp crackled over his headset as Teresa took a step back, tilting her head forward, hiding her face with the brim of Sherrie's hat.

"Just stay calm."

The man faced the doors, pressing the button for the ground level. He glanced back at her. "Teresa?"

Leroux cursed as did half the room, the other half gasping.

Teresa shook her head. "I don't speak Russian," she said in Russian with a thick Polish accent.

"You should learn if you're going to live here," said the man before turning back to face the doors. They reached the ground floor and he stepped off, the doors closing once again, the elevator continuing to the parking levels.

Tong leaned back, breathing a relieved sigh. "Thank God we're the only ones who heard that." She gestured at the monitors. "No reaction." The main display switched its focus to the parking garage cameras as soon as Teresa stepped off the elevator. She headed for Sherrie's SUV, the fob extended in front of her. She pressed the button and the lights flashed, and moments later she was inside and pulling away.

Leroux rose, leaning forward on his station, his knuckles pressed against the hard surface. Tong manipulated the main display, switching from camera to camera as she tracked Sherrie's vehicle. The window rolled down as Teresa approached the gate and she came to a halt. Her hand, gripping Sherrie's phone, extended toward the security reader and she leaned out, her hat catching on the window frame, tipping it back and revealing her face.

"Oh, hell no!" exclaimed Child as he threw his hands up in the air and spun in his chair.

Teresa's head jerked back inside and she adjusted the hat, placing her free hand on top to hold it in place as she leaned back out. The door rolled open and she pulled out as her window closed. The SUV climbed the ramp then turned left, merging into traffic.

Leroux snapped his fingers. "Replay that footage. I want to see if they actually got a clear shot of her face or if we're just imagining it."

"Still no reaction from the drones or the car," reported Packman. "But the guys inside are looking pretty hard at their tablets."

"I've got the footage," said Tong.

"Play it."

Tong played the footage and Leroux frowned. He could see Teresa's face, though it was only for a brief moment.

"I think we're in the clear," said Packman.

Leroux glanced over his shoulder at him. "You mean you don't see her face?"

"No, do you?"

"Plain as day."

"Just a sec." Tong tapped at her keyboard. The video played again, this time frame by frame. Everyone stared as Teresa slowly reached out of the car. Her hat caught on the window frame revealing her face before she darted back inside. But it wasn't as he had pictured. Her entire face wasn't revealed. All that was visible was from the nose down. The all-important eyes had remained hidden the entire time, his brain filling in what it knew from file photos.

"Told you," said Packman.

The tension in Leroux's shoulders eased and he leaned back, relieved. "Okay, we're all agreed then that her face wasn't revealed?"

A string of acknowledgments replied.

"Still no reaction from the Russians?"

"Negative," replied Tong. "I found a new camera angle from an ATM across the street. All four of them have stopped staring at their tablets and resumed whatever discussion they were having."

Leroux glanced at the time. "It's been five minutes. Sherrie should be leaving now."

Child pointed at the screen. "There, she's getting on the elevator."

Tong tapped a couple of keys and the feed showing the most important person in Leroux's life, expanded to fill most of the massive display.

"That got a reaction." Packman split the screen showing video of three of the men exiting the surveillance vehicle and sprinting down the sidewalk toward the entrance of Teresa's building.

"Holy shit!" exclaimed Child. "This is actually happening!"

Leroux pressed his forefinger hard against his lips and momentarily closed his eyes.

Please, God, help her get out of this.

Novikov Residence

Moscow, Russia

Sherrie leaned against the rear of the elevator, her head slightly turned away from the camera mounted in a corner behind her. There would have been no avoiding it as she boarded, though she kept her exposure to a minimum, scratching her forehead before immediately turning away from the camera and selecting the ground floor then stepping back against the wall. If she had comms, she'd know exactly what was going on, what to expect. Her intention was to walk out the main lobby and onto the street, then hang a left in the opposite direction of where the surveillance vehicle was set up. Once out of sight of the drones and their controllers, she'd hail a cab to get out of the area then make the rendezvous with Teresa. But for all she knew, the doors could open and the four-man team could be standing there, waiting for her, guns drawn.

The elevator chimed as it passed the second floor, and the ground floor light lit up. She pushed off the wall with her bum and drew a breath, preparing her reaction for whatever might come. The elevator car came to a halt with a jerk and the doors opened. She exhaled in relief to find two residents standing there and no team sent to arrest her. She stepped off, smiling pleasantly at the couple who then boarded, and she strode casually toward the main entrance and the natural light flowing through the floor-to-ceiling glass. As she approached the doors, her heart picked up a few extra beats as she spotted three men sprinting up the steps.

Shit. Of course this wasn't going to be easy.

She continued as if they could not possibly have anything to do with her. She pulled open the door and stepped outside as the men skidded to a halt, surrounding her. One of them flashed his badge.

"FSB. Teresa Novikov, you're coming with us."

Sherrie, eyes narrowed, looked up at the man. "Who the hell is Teresa Novikov?"

The man's eyes shot wide and his jaw dropped slightly as he finally got a proper look at her face. "Who are you?"

"None of your business. I've done nothing wrong. You've obviously mistaken me for someone else. So, if you don't mind, get out of my way. I have places to go."

The man didn't budge. He reached out and pinched the sleeve of her jacket, giving it a shake. "Where did you get this?"

"My jacket?"

"Yes."

"At the Levsha Flea Market last year on clearance. They had a bunch of them."

He frowned and she gave him a look.

"I don't think it's your style."

"Watch your mouth. We're FSB. What were you doing in the building?"

"Visiting a friend."

"Who?"

"What business is that of yours?"

"Answer the question."

"This is the problem with Russia. No wonder so many people are leaving with goons like you running around. Her name is Anna Belsky, apartment eleven-oh-one. Now, are we done here?" She delivered a hacking cough. "You might want to stand back. I think I'm about to have a fit." She coughed again.

"What's wrong with you?"

"According to my doctor, tuberculosis. I must have caught it at the damn restaurant. I was supposed to be in treatment this afternoon, but that's not going to happen with all this harassment." She coughed again then bit the inside of her cheek, drawing blood. She spat and held up the bloody mess. "I guess the doctor's right."

All three men took a rapid step back, the man she had been speaking to placing a hand in front of his mouth and nose. "You can go."

"Thank you." She continued to cough as she descended the steps, taking the left as planned. She didn't bother looking over her shoulder—it might make her appear suspicious. She ran her glove along a snow-covered railing then used what she collected to wash the spittle off her palm. She ran her tongue over the inside of her cheek and winced.

That's going to hurt for a while.

She would have to find water and a saltshaker. She just hoped it was healed up by the time she saw her boyfriend. She planned on banging the living shit out of him and didn't want any distractions.

Grey Network Safe House

Moscow, Russia

Jack peered through the peephole to see a young woman standing there. "Yowza." He had expected Thorn to send a man, but the spy game was equal opportunity. Then again, this might not be his contact. He opened the door slightly and peered out. She stared at him.

"Are you going to let me in?"

"And who are you?"

"A mutual friend sent me."

He grinned, stepping back and hauling the door open. "Well, why didn't you say so? Mutual friends are my most favorite kind."

She stepped inside carrying two large duffle bags. He closed the door behind her and before he had a chance to offer any help, she had both bags up on the table. She removed her winter jacket, revealing a fabulous figure that bulged in all the right places, and if it weren't for the fact the Russian government wanted him for assassinating their leader, he'd be tempted to James Bond with her. Unfortunately, it had been his experience that, no matter how irresistible he thought he was, few women responded well to a forced kiss.

It must have been a Sean Connery thing.

"Take off your shirt."

He grinned. "Okay, sweetheart, but before we get jiggy with it, what should I call you?"

"No names."

His grin spread at her firm tone. "Yes, mistress. You can call me Slave. My safe word is 'Tribbles.'"

She eyed him. "Tribbles?"

"You know, from Star Trek."

"Not a fan."

Jack leaned to his side, getting a better shot of her ass. "Nobody's perfect, but you're close to it."

She gestured at him. "Why is your shirt still on? Get it off. I was told you have injuries."

He frowned as he removed his shirt. "Let me guess, we're not about to buff every flat surface in this place?"

She gave him a look. "In your dreams."

He shrugged, tossing his shirt on the table. "You'd be surprised what's been in my dreams lately."

"Come closer so I can examine you."

He did as told. "You can see why I'm confused with all the sexy talk."

"If you think this is sexy talk, you Americans are an odd lot."

He dropped his pants and she looked up at him. He smiled down at her. "Don't get any ideas, sweetheart, but you might as well do a thorough examination. Maybe there's something down there I missed."

She grunted and began at his feet, working her way slowly up his right leg. "Now here's something you missed." Both hands were gripping his upper thigh.

"I've heard he's hard to miss."

Her hands quickly ran down his opposite leg before she gently pressed into the top of his right foot. "You've got some bruising here." He winced as she pressed harder. "Does that hurt?"

"Will you think less of me if I say yes?"

"Could you be serious for a minute?"

"It's not in my nature, but I'll try. Yes, it does hurt. Is it broken?"

"No, it just feels like a bruise. I don't think anything's broken. Kick anyone recently?"

"Apparently."

"You don't sound certain."

"Gorgeous, I have no idea what the hell's happened in the past thirty-six hours. You could tell me I fought off a horny ten-peckered billy goat and I wouldn't be able to call you the fool."

"Interesting." She rose to her knees, her face deliciously close to Jack Jr., then reached up and pulled down his underwear a few inches. He groaned as two fingers jabbed into his side, just under his waistband, and he flinched, jerking his hips away. "Looks like you were kicked here." She cupped his boys through his underwear and squeezed.

"Should I cough?"

"Do they hurt?"

"I find the pain comes and goes. I think you'll need to hold them a little bit longer." She let go and gave them a swat. He winced. "Okay, I deserved that."

She stood and continued her examination of his torso then his arms, neck, and scalp. "You definitely got into one hell of an altercation with a right-handed man. He landed some good blows, and you defended against some." She took his right hand and closely examined his fingers. "What's odd is there's no indication you fought back."

He clenched his fist then splayed his fingers, examining his knuckles. "They're used to delivering a lot of blows, but you're right. If I fought back, there should be some evidence of that."

She stepped back. "You can get dressed now."

He picked up his pants. "Are you sure? Maybe you want to test out my cardiovascular?"

"You just don't know when to quit."

"Quitting isn't in my nature either."

She folded her arms and gave him a look. "While I will admit you are gorgeous, I don't think I want to get into a relationship with a man who stands accused of assassinating the president."

"Who said anything about a relationship?"

She rolled her eyes. "What kind of a girl do you think I am?"

He stepped into his pants. "Someone my charms are wasted on, I guess."

She laughed, gesturing at Jack Jr. "Turn that outie into an innie, and you might have stood a chance."

He grinned. "Ah, so there's a special lady in your life?"

"Yes."

"And I suppose watching is out of the question."

"You truly are an American pig, aren't you?"

"Hey, in America we keep pigs as pets. They're adorable, and so am I."

Her eyes widened. "Are you serious?"

"Sad but true."

She indicated his pants. "Actually, don't put those on."

He grinned. "I got you curious, didn't I?"

She groaned. "No, but I have clothes here that actually fit and are stylish. What you've got on looks like a geriatric picked them out for a sixties theme party."

He stared down at the pants. "Yeah, I can't remember the last time I saw corduroy." He let go of the waist and they dropped around his ankles. He stepped back out of them as she unpacked both bags. She handed him socks, jeans, an undershirt, then a casual buttoned-down shirt.

"These should look good on you."

"Hey, I thought I was rocking the corduroys."

"Nobody rocks corduroys."

He shrugged as he put on the far more fashionable clothes while she continued to unpack, revealing more clothing plus winter gear, weapons, comms, phone, and various other sundries. He quickly inventoried everything, inspecting all the weapons and ammo, then activated the phone.

"Is anything missing?"

"No, I think you've thought of everything."

"Good." She indicated the phone. "My number is programmed in there under 'Nurse.' Call it and leave a message. I monitor it regularly."

"No direct line?"

"No. If you get caught, I don't want anything that leads back to me."

"Makes sense. Besides, your girlfriend might get jealous if a man starts calling, begging to see you."

She stepped forward and planted a kiss on him then patted his cheek. "I don't have a girlfriend, but I don't get in relationships with men who are going to be dead before the sun goes down."

He licked his lips, tasting the remnants of hers. "And I don't date eternal optimists."

She chuckled. "If you make it out of this alive, call me. I'll finish my examination."

He grinned. "I like the sound of that."

She smacked his ass and headed for the door. "Good luck."

"Thanks. I think I'll be needing it."

She left and he locked the door behind her. He sent a message to Thorn.

Resupply received.

The new phone vibrated a moment later.

Copy that. I hope you weren't too rough on the poor girl.

I'm sure I have no idea what you're talking about. Has my status changed?

I've made my report. I'm still waiting to hear. Gear up and stand by. I'm working on a new location that hasn't been previously compromised, just in case Washington doesn't believe in the benefit of the doubt.

Copy that. Standing by.

Jack put the phone down then organized his supplies, putting all the essentials in one bag, the stuff he could leave behind in a pinch in the other. Finished, he sat on the couch, a Makarov pistol sitting beside him.

A high-pitched noise erupted from the TV, demanding to be heard despite the fact he had the volume set low. He opened his eyes and leaned forward to see an alert displayed ordering all military, police, and reserve forces to report in immediately. If he couldn't discover the truth soon, the world would end believing he had triggered World War III.

And he refused to let that be his legacy.

Leaving Novikov Residence

Moscow, Russia

Sherrie stared out the window of her cab as she rapidly put some distance between her and Teresa's apartment building. If they had gotten away with it, she should be fine for the next short while. Eventually, they would hit the apartment, discover it empty, then start reviewing footage once again, but by then it would hopefully be too late. She would have reunited with Teresa and they would be in the underground railroad. But if suspicions had been raised, they could be following her right now, and if she attempted to lose them, it would only raise further suspicions.

Her watch pulsed, electricity tingling her wrist with an urgent message from Langley. She shifted in her seat, surreptitiously pressing the edge of the watch face in a coded pattern, then glanced at the scrolling message.

Drone has followed. Moscow recalling all civil and defense forces.

The message repeated and she pressed a combination clearing it from the watch, automatically sending an acknowledgment back to Langley that she had received the update. This was the worst-case scenario. They were one step away from all-out war, and the Russians would be responding accordingly. They would tighten security not only at the borders, but within Moscow. It would make getting Teresa out that much more difficult, and it would definitely mean she would be trapped here.

Or, if this thing did go south, with Moscow a primary target, she could die quickly but alone. If the world was ending, she wanted to die in the arms of the only man she had ever loved. She had a life planned out for them. Marriage, children. They were supposed to grow old together, but if things kept going the way they were, no one was growing old. She had often thought of whether she would want to survive some sort of worldwide calamity, whether that was a nuclear war, asteroid impact, or mass plague, and had come to the conclusion she would rather die with the masses. She wasn't the type that felt it was her duty to perpetuate the human race, to keep it going at all costs. And if 90% of it were wiped out, what was the point?

Living near Langley meant certain death in a nuclear war, but it meant nothing when it came to natural disasters or some sort of outbreak. There was no way to ensure they were going to die. She growled. How the hell was a girl supposed to make sure she avoided the apocalypse?

"Something wrong?" asked the cabbie.

She flinched, having momentarily forgotten her situation. She sighed with a frown then removed her hat, pointing at her hair. "This looks like a dog that's been caught out in the rain. I need to get my hair done. Do you know a place nearby that might not need an appointment?"

A finger raised off the steering wheel, pointing ahead. "My sister has a shop just up here." He grabbed his phone off the passenger seat and minutes later was dropping her off in front of a mall with an appointment to see Irina in five minutes. It was perfect. The mall would have multiple exits and she could lay low here while Langley coordinated an escape for her and Teresa.

All while the world went to hell.

Director Morrison's Office, CIA Headquarters

Langley, Virginia

"Sir, we've got a problem."

Morrison indicated for Leroux to take a seat and he did. He yawned and bit a knuckle. "You look like shit," said Morrison.

Leroux grunted, jerking his chin at his boss. "You don't look so good yourself, sir."

Morrison chuckled. "I don't think many people have had much sleep for the past twenty-four hours, and if things keep going the way they're going…" His voice trailed off. "Well, you know."

Leroux frowned. Everyone was worried, everyone was scared. DEFCON 2 was something few of them had gone through, and the Russians were on high alert, mobilizing all their forces and reserves. NATO was in a panic. Any conventional war would hit Western Europe first, especially the former Soviet States. But nuclear would affect them all. The question was, what do you do if it's a limited nuclear exchange?

If Russia were to launch and only take out military bases along their western border in countries that only a few short decades ago were enemies of the West, would that justify America launching its nukes, or England or France? According to Article 5 of the NATO Treaty, war on one was war on them all, but it didn't dictate what the response was. Take out the defensive capabilities of the Baltic Republics, of Poland, Hungary, Romania, and the former Czechoslovakia, but leave Germany, France, and the UK untouched, what did you do? NATO would automatically be at war and would likely commit conventional forces, but would they nuke Russia and risk all-out war? Mutually Assured Destruction continued to apply.

But with a leader now in power in Russia who believed that there was a distinction between strategic and tactical uses of nuclear weapons, had the game changed? Unfortunately, he feared it had. There was no longer a stomach for war, not in the West. He feared that if Russia did what its new president had promised before he had power, NATO's response would be to fortify their traditional territory, then use economic sanctions in an attempt to weaken Russia. And if they did, it would send a message to China that it was open season on whatever they wanted to take.

Leroux sighed heavily. "Sir, do you think this could be the end?"

Morrison leaned back, folding his arms, tapping his chin with the side of his index finger. "It could be, but I have a feeling it's only the beginning of the end. Washington is already trying to figure out what to do if the Russians do use tactical nukes. No one's going to destroy the world because Kyiv or Odesa are taken out."

"And that's the problem, isn't it? Once the Russians, and hell, the Chinese, figure that out, there'll be no stopping them."

Morrison agreed. "The world's a different place than it was in the sixties, even the eighties. What a lot of people in the West don't realize is that economies outside of our sphere of influence are massive now. If we were preoccupied in Europe and China decided to assert itself in their region, there'd be little we could do about it. And all they would have to do is sign non-aggression treaties with countries like India, South Korea, Japan, hell, even Australia, and various other mid-sized economies and create their own economic bloc that would carry them through any sanctions we might impose. They'd hurt for a little bit, but they'd eventually be fine, and the Chinese think in far longer terms than we do. If we're not careful, we could find ourselves standing alone against the bear and the dragon with Europe in ruin, a gutted manufacturing base, and former trading partners too scared to do business with us because we can no longer protect them. That scares me more than all-out war."

Leroux shifted in his chair. "Well, if I wasn't on edge before, I certainly am now."

Morrison laughed. "You asked. Now, what's this problem?"

"Teresa seems to have gotten away clean, and at first we thought Sherrie had as well, but the Russians I guess had their suspicions, so they sent one of their drones to follow her. I've been able to warn her, so she's holed up in a mall, but the drone is overhead monitoring the entrance. It buys her maybe an hour, but eventually, she's going to have to leave. There are other exits she can go out and she's good at her job, so we can hopefully get her out safely."

"Then what's the problem?"

"Teresa. She's refusing to be picked up by anyone else. She says she doesn't know who she can trust and she's unwilling to meet with an unfamiliar face."

"So, unless we can get Sherrie free and clear, the only person who knows what the hell the intel was that Jack was supposed to retrieve is refusing to cooperate."

"Exactly."

Morrison cursed. "Has she ever met with any of our other assets besides Sherrie?"

"Only one."

Morrison frowned. "Jack."

"Exactly. I take it since I haven't heard anything, you weren't successful in pleading his case?"

"No. While Washington agrees that he's probably innocent and being used in some way, they can't risk reversing their decision as long as the Russians are convinced he's involved. If we did anything to help him and they found out, that would be all the confirmation they would need that we were behind the assassination."

"Then what are we going to do? We need that intel. Teresa has already confirmed it has something to do with this situation."

"Then appeal to her better nature. If she doesn't give us that information, if she continues to refuse, she could be responsible for the end of humanity."

Leroux rose. "Let's hope that works, as this is one time I don't want to be able to say I told you so."

Thorn Residence

Vienna, Austria

Thorn stood on her small balcony, absentmindedly running her finger along the wrought iron railing, ridding it of the small pile of snow that had accumulated overnight. She stared down at the street below, her neighbor's notorious British sports car being jumped for the umpteenth time, its famously unreliable electrical system never able to stand up to even a mild Austrian winter. She shivered and stepped back inside, closing the door, then shuffled over to the fire, warming herself.

Her body was still racked with aches and pains from the beating. She would never recover fully. This endless torture would be all she would know for the rest of her days, but she had discovered that moving from the cold of the winter to the heat of a fire, provided some relief, if only for a few minutes. This recent revelation had her debating whether she should move to a more traditionally cold climate or install a standup freezer for when it wasn't winter. Her shoulders slumped as she took a step back from the fire, the heat too intense.

This isn't how I imagined retirement.

She was supposed to retire, spend her summers in her beloved Vienna, and her winters along the Mediterranean, contending with the normal travails of age. But this, this was something entirely different that she wasn't convinced she wanted to endure for perhaps decades to come. Her Langley-approved doctor wanted to put her on opioids, but she had seen what it could do to people and was extremely reluctant.

Her chin sagged into her chest and she squeezed her eyes shut as she pinched the bridge of her nose, fighting off the tears in a rare moment of self-pity. Her shoulders shook and she gasped, inhaling deeply as she opened her eyes and stared into the flames.

Maybe it's time to stop being a martyr.

Her phone rang. She stepped over to the table and picked it up.

Unknown caller.

She took the call. "Hello?"

"Do you recognize my voice?"

She did. It was Morrison. "Yes. What can I do for you?"

"We have a situation that only you can help with, but no one can know who asked you to help."

She smiled slightly, her suspicions confirmed. Jack was still disavowed, Washington unwilling to take any risks due to the current situation. But someone obviously recognized how valuable he was. She suspected that someone was Morrison himself. "What do you need?"

Grey Network Safe House

Moscow, Russia

Jack jerked awake as the unfamiliar ring of his new phone blared at him. He adjusted the volume of the ringer then answered the unknown caller.

"Da?"

"It's me."

He sat upright at Thorn's voice. "I was starting to wonder if you had abandoned me too."

"It'll be a cold day in hell before I ever abandon any of my people."

"Happy to hear it. So, have you got a safe house for me?"

"I do, but I need you to make a stop along the way."

His eyebrows rose. "Oh? I have a face that isn't exactly welcome on the streets of Moscow."

"Unfortunately, we're going to have to take that risk. I need you to pick up an asset that refuses to come in with anybody but a familiar face."

"Who?"

"An old friend of yours from Warsaw or, more accurately, who you last saw in Warsaw."

An eyebrow shot up. "Teresa?"

"Exactly."

"So, she's all right?"

"Depends on what your definition of all right is. From what I've been told, she left your hotel room, returned to her own, then reported for work the next day where she met with Director Nikitin, was questioned, then sent back to Moscow where she was interrogated, then let go after the assassination. She returned to her apartment and Sherrie White was sent in to meet with her. Unfortunately, the FSB was monitoring her. We managed to get her out, but Sherrie's being followed, so can't make the rendezvous, and Teresa's refusing to meet with any other CIA personnel."

"I don't blame her, what with everything that's going on. So, Langley wants me to go in?"

"No, you're still disavowed. However, a certain chief that we know and love has called in a personal favor with me to see if there's anything I can do to help."

Jack grinned. "So, if you read between the lines…"

"Exactly. You are how I'm going to help. I'm sending you the address of the safe house that you're going to take her to, and her current location. She's in an underground parking garage about fifteen minutes away from you by city bus."

"My face is everywhere. There's no way I'm traveling on public transit without someone recognizing me. I'll borrow a car."

"Use the tricks of the trade in your care package. You'll be fine. Pick up Teresa, get to the safe house, then we'll figure out what to do from there."

"Roger that." He rose and headed for the table, grabbing the small bag Thorn had referred to, and headed for the bathroom.

"Contact me when you're safe."

"Will do. Now, I'm going to let you go. We don't have a lot of time and it ain't easy making something so pretty unrecognizable."

Thorn laughed. "Good luck, Jack. We'll talk to you soon."

The call ended and Jack stared into the bathroom mirror. "Damn these cheek bones."

Crocus City Mall

Moscow, Russia

Sherrie stared at herself in the mirror. "Damn, Irina, you do good work. I'm definitely coming back here."

Irina beamed at her. "I'm so happy to hear that." She held up her phone. "Can I take a photo for my portfolio?"

Sherrie rose, shaking her head. "I'm sorry, I'm in such a hurry. I didn't have time for this but it was necessary. Next time, I promise, you can take all the photos you want."

Irina shrugged, stuffing her phone back in her apron. Sherrie paid in cash then gave Irina a quick hug. "Thanks again, dear. And thank your brother for me. He saved my life."

Irina laughed. "I'll tell him. He's single, you know."

Sherrie chuckled. "Unfortunately for him, I'm not."

"He'll be devastated."

"He'll get over it." Sherrie left the salon and headed deeper into the mall. She spotted a kiosk where she bought a new prepaid phone, then headed for the food court where she grabbed a Grand De Luxe combo at Tasty and That's It, the pale imitation of what was once McDonald's before it pulled out of this forsaken country. She sat in a corner, away from the crowds, and activated her phone as she chowed down on the poor substitute. She took a long drag of her soda, her fries heavily over-salted. Her phone indicated a successful activation and she wiped her hands and mouth before pairing a set of wireless earbuds. She dialed a long-memorized local access number as she pushed them into her ears.

The call was immediately answered. "This is the operator."

"This is Skylark, access code Sierra-Hotel-Four-Two-Seven-Eight-Five-One. Request connect to Control."

"Stand by, Skylark."

There was a clicking sound and a moment later the familiar beep of a call transfer. Leroux answered. "I was wondering when we would hear from you."

She smiled. "Sorry, I was busy. I had to get my hair done."

There was a pause. "Are you serious?"

She resumed eating her fries. "Hey, your message indicated I was being watched. I had to lay low so I got my hair done."

"Where are you now?"

"I'm in the food court of the mall. I assume you know which mall."

"We do."

"I'm just eating what is truly McDog food. Am I still being watched?"

"Yes. There's a drone monitoring the front entrance. We have to assume they're definitely still interested in you. They just hit the apartment five minutes ago, so I have no doubt the heat on you is going to increase as soon as they review the footage and see that you came from her floor. We need to get you out of there now."

As she listened, she rapidly scarfed down the rest of the food. Even though it wasn't tasty by her standards, it was calories that would give her energy for what was to come. At this moment, she had no idea when she'd get another chance to eat. "What's the plan?" she mumbled as she chewed.

"First, you have to lose that jacket. You stand out like a sore thumb in it."

She eyed it, sitting on the back of the chair beside her. "Done."

"Then go out the rear entrance. We haven't spotted any drones, but they could be monitoring surveillance cameras. Get a hat and scarf so you can cover your features as best you can. If they recognize you coming out, they'll redeploy the drone from the front. If they don't, then we'll know. I'm dispatching someone from Moscow Station to collect you. What's the ETA on her ride?"

"Seven minutes," replied Tong in the background.

"ETA is seven minutes."

"Copy that." She ate her last fry then drained her drink. "Anything else I need to know? How's Teresa?"

"Refusing to cooperate. She only wants to be picked up by you."

"Well, you can't blame her for that. Tell my ride to plan out a route to collect her."

"Negative, that's no longer your mission. Right now, we need to get you secure. We'll reevaluate if you make it out clean."

She frowned but he was right. They had to be certain she wasn't followed, otherwise, she would lead them directly to Teresa. "Acknowledged. I'm heading out now. I've got to buy a winter jacket."

"Can you stay on comms?"

"Yes, I'm using some knockoff AirPods." She policed her garbage then rose, emptied her tray into the garbage bin, then placed the hardened plastic on the pile. She left the food court and headed down the escalator, having already anticipated the need to replace her jacket, spotting a clothing store earlier. She picked out a knee-length one with a fur-lined hood, dark gray, nothing that would stand out, and surreptitiously hung her old jacket on the rack. She purchased a black scarf and winter hat, then quickly headed for the rear entrance, bundling up against the cold and the cameras. "I'm leaving now."

"Copy that. We're monitoring."

She pushed through the double doors then headed down the steps then left. She set a brisk but reasonable pace, matching that of those who had places to be, rather than those sauntering along for pleasure. "Report."

"The drone is holding position. No evidence they spotted you. Keep heading in the direction you are until you reach the next set of lights, then hang a left. ETA two minutes. Black Toyota sedan. Last three digits of the license plate, four-four-two."

"Four-four-two, copy that." Her heart was hammering. She struggled to control it. The police presence was heavy and military vehicles rolled past far too frequently. This was as heavy as she had ever seen Moscow security, and she got the sense it would only get worse. They were determined to get their hands on Jack, and she had little doubt word would go out to pick up Teresa and her accomplice. Unlike the Russian, she had the advantage that her face wasn't on camera. They could only put out a description, the most distinctive part of that being the jacket she had used and now abandoned.

If the Russians put two and two together and figured out she was involved, then she had little doubt the three men that had seen her face would be put in front of computers, reviewing every photo of every female they suspected to be an enemy agent, along with everyone who had arrived at any major border crossing in the past forty-eight hours. It could seriously hamper her ability to assist in the situation.

She reached the traffic lights and hung a left. Her eyes scanned the traffic ahead and she spotted a black sedan pulling up to the curb. Rather than blindly climb in like too many fake Uber victims, she confirmed the plate. "I've got the car."

"Confirmed," said Leroux. "That's it. Get in the back like it's a taxi."

She did as told, closing the door and breathing a sigh of relief at the tinted windows. The car immediately pulled away from the curb and the driver glanced in his rear-view mirror.

"My instructions are to bring you to a safe house about ten minutes from here unless I am told different." He reached over to the passenger seat then handed her fresh comms. "I've got a gift for you."

She smiled at the man. "Thanks. Stand by, Control, I'm switching to comms."

"Copy that."

She removed the earbuds then ended the call on her phone. She fit the tiny device into her ear canal then pressed twice on her ear to activate it. "Control, Skylark, can you read, over?"

"We read you, Skylark."

"Status?"

"The drone is still holding position at the front entrance. It looks like you made a clean getaway."

"Good. We need to arrange a switch just in case they eventually do figure it out, and then I'm going to collect Teresa."

"Agreed. Keep heading for the safe house. We'll make arrangements for a second vehicle in a location where you can lose the cameras. I'm going to let Teresa know that you're on your way."

"Copy that. And I'm going to need a resupply. I can't return to my hotel, so I'm going to need clothes, weapons, everything."

"We'll arrange it."

"Good, and we're going to need new faces. Have Moscow Station print off one for me and one for Teresa. We need to be able to move freely. We'll need IDs to match."

"Will do."

"Any word on Jack?"

"Only that there's no change in his status."

She muttered a curse. "Understood. Then I guess I'm on my own."

"Not as long as I'm in your ear."

She smiled. "I'd say I wish you were here, but with everything going on, that would sound rather hateful, wouldn't it?"

The love of her life chuckled. "Then I'll say it for us. I wish *you* were *here*."

"Something's going on," called a voice in the background.

"Stand by, Skylark."

Sherrie tensed, her head on a swivel as she peered out the windows. "Keep your eyes open," she warned the driver. "Something's going on."

"My eyes are always open."

Leroux reported. "Half a dozen police vehicles just pulled up to the mall and at least a dozen officers went inside."

She cursed. "They probably figured out what cab I got into, contacted him, and he told them I was getting my hair done by his sister. All right, we don't have much time. If I can't collect Teresa and get her to a safe location in the next twenty minutes, the Russians are going to start arresting every blonde they see." She glanced behind her at the sound of a siren. "Prove to me why your team's the best."

"Consider it done."

Express Secure Parking

Moscow, Russia

Teresa sat in the American agent's SUV, trembling. She had been on plenty of ops during her career, but they were usually fairly tame. She was sent into a nightclub or casino or some event, dressed provocatively, there to seduce someone so they could then be blackmailed or otherwise coerced into giving information. Depending on who the target was, yes, it could be dangerous, but she had never feared for her life until today. Her country was after her. A country, if the radio was to be believed, now led by a madman hell-bent on restoring the Soviet Union to a former glory it never possessed.

The Americans were still in her ear, and for almost an hour had been telling her nothing she wanted to hear. The American agent, Sherrie, had been believed compromised and couldn't make the rendezvous with everything going on. She didn't know whom to trust, and right now, tucked away in a parking garage where there were no cameras, she was certain she was far safer here than with some unknown agent.

Unfortunately, there was only one person she trusted, and that was Jack, and he was out of the picture permanently. She had no idea what to do. Security was only growing tighter in the city, the rhetoric emerging from the Kremlin becoming more volatile. Soon, she would have no choice but to trust the Americans.

Her shoulders slumped as she squeezed her eyes shut, battling the temptation to cry in frustration. With the benefit of hindsight, she should have insisted on extraction rather than the exchange with Jack in Warsaw. It had simply never occurred to her that it would come to this. The Americans were supposed to receive the intel, have time to act on it, and prevent what had happened. Never in her wildest dreams would she have imagined Jack would somehow be implicated in the assassination of the president, nor that her own government would suspect her involvement as well.

The comms beeped in her ear and she flinched, unaccustomed to the state-of-the-art gear. "Red Sonja, Control. Do you read, over?"

Her heart raced. "Confirmed, Control, I read you."

"We have good news. Skylark is clear for the moment. She's on her way to collect you. ETA fifteen minutes."

She smiled and her entire body relaxed, if only for a moment. "That's good news, Control. I assume you have an extraction plan."

"It's being put together as we speak. We'll have you to a safe house in less than an hour, then into the underground railroad as quickly as possible. There could be some delays, however, due to the tightening security in Moscow."

"Understood."

She checked her watch. Fifteen minutes. But that was an estimate. It could be ten, it could be twenty. Hell, it could be an hour if something went wrong. "Keep me posted at five-minute intervals on her ETA."

"Roger that, five-minute intervals."

Movement in the mirrors caught her eye and she sat up from her crouched position, her heart leaping into her throat at the sight of a vehicle parked behind her, blocking her in. "Something's wrong," she said, panic in her voice.

"What?"

"Somebody's just blocked me in. Could she be here early?"

"Negative, Red Sonja. Skylark is nowhere near you. Are you armed?"

She fumbled for her purse, reaching inside and gripping her weapon. "Yes."

"Be prepared to defend yourself, but don't overreact. We don't know what's going on yet."

A door opened behind her and a figure emerged. She could only see their waist. It was a man, slim build. He rounded her rear bumper, now on her side. She gripped her weapon, her finger on the trigger guard, and pressed it against her stomach, keeping it hidden, the barrel aimed up at the window. There was a tap on the glass and she leaned away from it slightly, adjusting her aim as the man bent down.

"I'd appreciate it if you didn't shoot me. I'm quite fond of the number of holes I already have."

She cried out in relief at Jack's smiling face. She lowered her gun. "It's Jack!"

"Can you repeat that, Red Sonja?"

"It's Jack!" She was giggling, her nerves getting the better of her.

He tapped again on the window. "Open the door. We've got to get out of here."

She grabbed her few things off the passenger seat and unlocked the door. He opened it and helped her out. They both climbed into his vehicle, pulling away moments later.

"Red Sonja, report your status," repeated Control in her ear, the man's voice growing more urgent as she continued to ignore him, more focused on Jack's arrival.

"I'm with Jack. We're in his car. We're leaving the parking garage now."

Jack glanced at her. "You're on comms?"

She tapped her ear.

"Ask them if they're still barred from communicating with me."

Control responded without her asking. "Tell him he's still disavowed. All communications officially have to go through you. Where is he taking you?"

Teresa frowned. "They say you're still disavowed. All communications have to go through me. They want to know where you're taking me."

"Somewhere safe and completely off the books. We'll contact them when we get there." He nodded toward her ear. "Now deactivate that thing. I don't want anybody to be able to track us."

She did as told, Control protesting until he was cut off. "Done. Is there a reason you're cutting your own people out of the loop?"

Jack pulled out of the parking garage and turned onto the street. "Yep." He merged into traffic, saying nothing more, and she twisted in her seat.

"And are you going to share that reason?"

"Actually, there are reasons. One is that right now, Russia thinks that America, through me, killed their leader. While I may have done it, I'm quite certain my country had nothing to do with it. So, minimal communications between them and me is the safest thing for now. If the Russians were to detect our conversation, they would take it as confirmation that I was still under their control and I had executed their orders."

It made sense. Everything on the news indicated her country was convinced the Americans were behind this, and the news she had been listening to while waiting for Sherrie indicated Russia was already suggesting it was an act of war, and was weighing its options. If she were the Americans, she'd be making certain every elected official from the president on down was secure. The least provocative response her country could employ would be to assassinate the American president. A tit for tat response, no conventional warfare, no nuclear weapons. "You said there were reasons, plural."

"I don't know who to trust. Very few people knew I was in Warsaw, yet I was targeted at the embassy."

"How do you know it was you and not me?"

"Because you weren't the one being set up to assassinate the president. I saw the video. If that's not me, they had somebody with my build already training to duplicate my gait, and they were ready to put my face in there somehow. They were targeting me the entire time, so the question is, how did they find out about the meeting, and the real question here is who's actually behind this? Let's think about this fresh. You stumbled upon a piece of intel that has you so concerned, you demanded an immediate meeting with me. Now, I still have no idea what the hell that intel was, so why don't you tell me what had you so concerned?"

She regarded him for a moment. Her deal with the Americans was that she wouldn't share her knowledge of the intel until she was safely out of the country, but perhaps it was time to stop thinking of just herself and instead concern herself with the risk to the world. "There was a briefing note that indicated a high probability that the American government was going to assassinate our president within the next few days in the hopes that someone more moderate would replace him, thus ending the Ukrainian situation and any future threats to Western Europe."

Jack pursed his lips as he guided them through traffic. "That's ridiculous."

She shrugged. "Yet here we are with the president dead and you, an American, accused of it."

Jack grunted. "Yeah, I suppose you're right." He glanced over at her. "How did you come across this?"

"It was on the bottom of a stack of files."

His eyes narrowed. "What?"

"Some files were delivered to my office. One of the files had a paperclip that another file got caught on. I noticed it, read it, and realized how important it was."

"So, you actually think that a file that important was accidentally paperclipped to the back of your file?"

She frowned. "What are you suggesting?"

"I'm suggesting you were set up."

"Impossible."

"Impossible? Look at what happened in Warsaw. I was targeted at the embassy and drugged. You were probably supposed to be drugged as well. After I passed out in the hotel room, somebody obviously collected me and brought me to Moscow, and either somehow convinced me to assassinate the president, or made it look like I did, faking all the injuries that would have been received during such an attempt."

"But why target me?"

He shrugged. "They obviously had made some sort of connection between the two of us. They suspect who I might actually be, so drop a piece of intel on you they knew you couldn't ignore. We arrange the meet, they're obviously monitoring your comms somehow, and that puts their plan in motion."

"But why? Couldn't they just grab you and do it anyway? Or grab anyone?"

He shook his head. "No, they need this to be believable to the world. They figured out you're a double agent. They trigger you with a piece of intel that describes exactly what they plan to do. You make contact with whoever your handler is, you immediately request assignment to Warsaw, they send in a team. Hell, Director Nikitin was even there. They see who you make contact with, and that's me at the gala. I'm drugged then taken from the hotel and framed. They then have on video a meeting between you and me at the embassy, probably video of us arriving together at the hotel, and then the intel itself claiming that an American was going to assassinate the president. They'll release all this information in the next day or so showing that it was a conspiracy between agents of the FSB and suspected agents of the CIA."

"But if that's the case, why did they let me go?"

"They didn't. They put you out there as bait to try to catch me, probably. Remember, I wasn't supposed to escape."

"But then doesn't that mean your government isn't involved? It's mine?"

He shrugged. "It's just a theory. We need to hole up where we can think." He pointed at a group of soldiers gathering on a sidewalk. "We don't have a lot of time. This city's going to go into lockdown, and if we don't figure out what's going on soon, it'll be too late."

Operations Center 3, CIA Headquarters

Langley, Virginia

Tong stared at Leroux. "I can't believe he cut us off."

Neither could Leroux. Jack was a bit unorthodox. Hell, he was a lot unorthodox, but it was one of the things that made him such a great officer. Doing the unexpected was exactly what was expected of him, and cutting off his only lifeline, even if it were through Teresa, was certainly unexpected.

Leroux had thought Jack would want to take advantage of any possible means of communication with those in this room. He was obviously concerned about something. Could he suspect a leak? Could he suspect Agency involvement? It wouldn't be unprecedented. In the eighties, there was a conspiracy between rogue KGB and CIA assets to assassinate Gorbachev. Director Morrison had helped foil the attempt and history had played out as it should. Could someone have gone rogue again? Could some cabal within the CIA or some other branch of the

American government grown frustrated with the situation in Russia, with its interference and outright hostility, and had felt forced to act?

The Russians had interfered in Syria, Libya, and now Ukraine. Should they be victorious, Moldova was certainly next, then perhaps the Baltic states and other former Russian republics. By taking the Russian president out, they could be rolling the dice, hoping someone more moderate took over and brought Russia back onto the path toward democracy and integration into the world of liberal democracies. It was a stretch. A long stretch. He couldn't believe that people would be naïve enough to think that the person who would replace the Russian president would be a moderate. The briefing he had read indicated that General Kalishnik, who had now laid claim to power with the blessing of a terrified Duma, was exactly who the analysts had expected would take power should an event like this play out. As far as he could see, there were two important questions that needed to be answered. One was whether the man was all talk, the other was whether he was behind the assassination.

"What are you thinking?"

He regarded Tong, the person he trusted the most in the building. "I think he either suspects Agency involvement, or he's protecting his country by limiting communications between a suspected assassin and us."

Child spun in his chair, staring up at the ceiling. "Do you really think we could be involved?"

Leroux sighed, facing him. "Anything's possible. There is a school of thought that eliminating leaders like that should be considered. The problem is the alternative could be worse."

Child dropped his foot, killing his spin. "You mean like if you had a time machine and could go back and kill Hitler or prevent him from being born, should you?"

"Exactly. World War Two was horrible. Tens of millions of people died, but it led to peace in Western Europe for over 70 years. There were incredible scientific advancements, not the least of which is the modern rocket program. If the war had never happened, could there have been a worse one later that killed more? There's no way to know, which is why we don't go around assassinating world leaders." His phone beeped on his desk and he picked up the receiver. "Leroux."

"Director Morrison wants to see you immediately."

"On my way." He hung up and rose. "The Chief wants to see me. Let me know the moment you reestablish contact with Teresa or Jack."

"Will do," replied Tong.

Leroux headed for Morrison's office, his mind still racing. He refused to believe his government was involved, however, it didn't mean that Americans weren't. He didn't know Jack very well, but knew him well enough to trust that he would always do what he thought was best for his country. The question was whether Jack thought assassinating the Russian president was what was best. He could have done it willingly, and now just be lying.

He refused to believe that as well. Jack was intelligent, extremely intelligent, and he would know the risks were too great. And there was another important fact that would be ignored in a court of law but was extremely relevant. The one piece of evidence linking Jack to the assassination was the video, and the only part of that video that incriminated him was the part that showed him looking up at the camera. Someone like Jack would never make a mistake like that.

Leroux was ushered into Morrison's office, still deep in thought. He took a seat on autopilot then finally looked up when Morrison cleared his throat.

"Penny for your thoughts?"

Leroux grunted. "Not sure they're worth even that, sir. Jack's collected Teresa somehow and cut off all communications with us. I think he suspects a leak on our end."

Morrison chuckled. "Well, there is a leak and I'm it. I reached out to Thorn and had Jack collect Teresa when it looked like Sherrie was compromised."

Leroux smirked. "Well, that explains that, but I don't think that's the kind of leak he's thinking of."

Morrison regarded him. "What's that famous gut telling you? It's onto something, I can tell."

Leroux pursed his lips, shaking his head slowly. "That's just it, sir. I still have no idea what's going on though something did occur to me after Teresa revealed that the intel did have something to do with the current situation."

Morrison leaned forward. "Go on."

"Well, the intel would have to deal with the assassination, wouldn't it?"

"I would think so."

"Then if it did, the question is, how did she get her hands on it? The assassination of the Russian president is about as serious a piece of intel as you can get. She's a low-level operative. They mostly use her to sleep with high-value targets so they can get some compromising video. She's not exactly the type of asset they would involve in investigating a plot to murder the president."

Morrison leaned back, folding his arms. "That's true. And something like that isn't exactly left lying around."

"No."

"Are you suggesting they're using her, or that she's been playing us?"

"I think she's being played. I think they slipped her the intel because they knew she was a double agent. It's so juicy, she reaches out to her handler, which is Jack, and arranges a meet. Because they suspect she's working for the other side, they've got her closely monitored, and as soon as they know the meet's in Warsaw, they set everything up. They nab her contact, which they know will be CIA, then set up the frame job."

Morrison tapped his chin. "So then Jack wasn't the target?"

"Not specifically, no. It was whoever she met with, which would explain why they're using the wrong name. They actually don't know who he is, at least not initially. I'm guessing they've run his photo against their databases and have discovered he's a regular visitor, but his cover's solid. They likely don't yet suspect he's Agency."

"Okay. If we assume you're right about this, what does that tell us?"

"I'm not sure, but it does make me wonder about one thing."

"What's that?"

"If the Russians are involved in assassinating their own president, and they set Teresa up to be a patsy, why did they set her free?"

"What do you mean?"

"Well, we've been assuming they let her go to see if she would lead them to somebody, or make contact with Jack since he escaped the hotel. But if they're the ones behind the assassination and not her, then why would they risk letting her go?"

Morrison stared at him. "Wait a minute, what are you suggesting?"

"I'm suggesting, sir, that maybe whoever let her go isn't involved, and is trying to figure out the same thing we are."

Morrison smiled slightly. "So then, there might actually be some Russians on our side."

"If it's true, sir, we need to find out who they are so we can enlist their help."

Director Nikitin's Office, FSB Headquarters

Moscow, Russia

"Sir, the president's office just called again."

Director Nikitin rolled his eyes. "What did you tell them?"

"Like you instructed me, sir, I said you were still out and I didn't know when you would be back."

"Good. Just keep telling them that."

"Sir, may I speak to you in private?"

He frowned. Katarina had been his secretary for three years. She was good at her job, pleasant to look at, and was a terrific stress reliever, his wife having lost interest in sex years ago. He loved her but had needs. Girls like Katarina filled the physical but could never satisfy the emotional ones. Those were handled by his wife, who he was certain had no doubt what was going on and with whom, though didn't seem to care as long as it was all kept behind closed doors.

The key to maintaining this arrangement was that the women he slept with never misinterpreted where they stood. There was no emotional relationship, purely physical, and the moment they developed feelings for him, he ended it. His typical secretary lasted about a year, Katarina being the exception. Three years was a record because she didn't seem to care. She merely sensed when he needed her, took care of business, then either left the office or returned to her room if they were on a business trip.

The perfect mistress.

But he didn't have time for her right now, yet she rarely misread the room. He found it hard to believe she wanted to see him for a quickie.

"Fine, come in."

The line disconnected and a moment later the door opened. Katarina stepped in, closing it behind her, her form-hugging miniskirt having him rethinking whether he could use a little diversion right now.

"What is it?"

She sat on one of the chairs in front of his desk and pulled closer before leaning forward and lowering her voice. "I'm concerned."

He regarded her. "About?"

"The president's office has called half a dozen times today and you ignored them every time."

He raised a finger. "Only the last two calls have been from the president's office. All the previous ones were from a man who laid claim to the president's office. Until that man is officially sworn in as president, I'm not answerable to him. I'm answerable to his predecessor or the chain of succession named by the Duma. General Kalishnik is certainly not the president's successor according to the laws we've all taken a vow to enforce."

"But now he *is*. I've been hearing in the media that all agency heads are pledging their allegiance to him, and those who don't are being arrested."

"I've heard the same reports, which is why I must avoid speaking to them for as long as possible."

Her eyes bulged. "You don't plan on swearing your allegiance?"

He vehemently shook his head. "That man will at best destroy this country, at worst destroy the entire planet. He is a madman convinced that the former Soviet Union should be reestablished, no matter what the cost. He's embraced the nonsense that the West is weak and can be defeated. NATO is not a paper tiger and our economy can't withstand further sanctions. If we were to do as he says, we would lose our only allies. While China and India might buy our oil today at steeply discounted prices, if we started a global war, their monetary support would disappear very quickly once the West informed their governments that they were being cut off for supporting the enemy. And when people like General Kalishnik think they're going to lose, they commit desperate acts, and could launch our arsenal. If he can't have the world then no one can."

Katarina paled as she listened to his assessment of the situation. "Then what are we going to do?"

"The FSB is one of the most powerful organizations in the country. He won't have total control as long as we hold out. In the meantime, we need to determine who assassinated the president."

"I thought the Americans did."

"No, the Americans aren't fools. They had nothing to do with this, I'm sure."

"Then who?"

He stared at her. If this went bad, if Kalishnik sent his men to arrest and ultimately execute him, would their new leader exact petty vengeance against this poor woman for not putting through his calls? "I think it's quite obvious who's behind it."

"You mean General Kalishnik?"

He nodded. "He has to be the one. The problem is proving it."

"Is that even possible?"

He sighed. "I don't know, but every hour that goes by, it becomes less and less so. We need help."

She stared at him, puzzled. "Help? But we're the FSB."

He inhaled deeply. "No, we *were* the FSB. Now we're split. There are those within the organization that believe as Kalishnik does, others who don't. If I issue an order from this office, and one of those loyal to Kalishnik finds out, they'll report to the Kremlin immediately and I'll be arrested as a traitor."

"Then who can help us?"

He sighed, turning in his chair and staring at the Russian flag that he had once been so proud of. "I fear the only people who can help us now are the Americans."

Thorn-Arranged Safe House

Moscow, Russia

Jack twisted the knob on the apartment door, finding it unlocked as promised. He stepped inside first, his head pivoting from left to right, finding it empty. He moved aside, letting Teresa enter, then peered out into the hallway, making certain no one had seen them enter. He closed the door and locked it.

Teresa pointed at the kitchen counter. "Here's the key."

He grabbed it and stuffed it in his pocket then quickly cleared the apartment. It was a one-bedroom hole in the wall, far less inviting than the accommodations he had coopted from the Grey Network, but it would do. They weren't here on a spa retreat. They were here to avoid the Russian authorities and to find some time to think.

Teresa sat on the couch, curling her legs up under her as Jack checked his two duffle bags transported here by someone. He guessed it was his sexy nurse. "What do we do now?"

"We prep as if we're leaving here in two minutes. Go use the bathroom, even if you don't think you need to. Do whatever it is you have to do in there." He pointed at her ear. "And reactivate the comms. Don't tell them where we are, though they'll pinpoint that the moment you go live. Just tell them that we've reached the safe house. We're secure for the moment and have minimal supplies. And request an update on your extraction."

She rose, heading for the bathroom as she reactivated her comms. He dialed Thorn and his handler picked up on the first ring.

"Status?"

"Good to hear from you too."

She chuckled. "Fine. How are you?"

"Lovely. You?"

"Delightful, until one of my people decided to make himself the most wanted man in the world."

He grinned. "I was always the most wanted man in the world, just for different reasons."

She groaned. "That ego of yours rivals even Kane's."

"It's only ego if it's not true. Now, as to your question, we've reached the safe house, though I'm only giving it two stars on Yelp. This is a real shit hole. The Grey Network knows how to treat its people."

"The Grey Network is working with more than an hour's notice."

"Excuses, excuses. I assume it was your girl who got my supplies transferred over. Thank her for me."

"Please don't bang her and break her heart."

"What kind of a guy do you think I am?"

"Exactly the kind of guy who lives by the credo, wham, bam, thank you, ma'am."

"I would never call her a ma'am. She's more of a thanks for the bliss, miss, type."

"Uh-huh. Just try to keep it in your pants until we prevent World War Three."

"Fine, but one way or the other I'm going out with a bang."

"I have no doubt. What's the status on your contact?"

"She's in the bathroom. She's reestablishing comms with Control."

"They're still refusing to talk to you?"

"Yep."

She sighed. "I guess you can't really blame them. I don't know if you've had a chance to check the news, but pretty much every armed forces in the world is on full alert, and everybody's scrambling to reposition whatever they can to send a message to Russia's new leadership that bullshit won't be tolerated. The UN Security Council has called an emergency meeting, and pretty much every Russian ambassador around the world has been called in. Unfortunately, none of those ambassadors know what the hell's going on, and they're starting to resign in droves. Some of them are even requesting asylum because they were supporters of the former regime. Things are falling apart fast. Eventually Langley will give in, but I'm afraid by the time they do, it'll be too late."

Jack cursed. "This is ridiculous. I need to be out there doing something, not holed up in some shit hole scratching my balls. I need a new face."

"And just what would you do?"

Jack opened his mouth to respond when he realized he didn't know what the hell he would do.

"Exactly. You can't go off half-cocked out there. You need a plan. Take this time to figure it out. I'll work on Langley."

Jack flashed a toothy smile at no one. "I'd go back to the hotel that I woke up in."

There was a pause. "Why would you do that?"

"Somebody put me in that room. Somebody saw something. We need to figure out who the hell kidnapped me from Warsaw. Once we find the minions, they'll lead us back to Gru."

"Who?"

"Doesn't matter. The bigwig behind this. This was too well-coordinated. I'm convinced now that they were aware Teresa was playing both sides and used her to make contact with me, though I'm not convinced they were after me specifically, just any American asset that they could then frame. They had agents at the embassy in Warsaw, then at my hotel. They were able to get me out of there, I assume without Langley being aware, get me on a plane to Moscow and into a hotel, all while keeping me knocked out, recreating the injuries and framing me for murder. That's not a couple of guys with a grudge. That's a well-coordinated, well-financed op, military or intelligence community, either current or former. This has General Kalishnik written all over it. Like I said, I need a new face and new ID so I can get out there and start cracking skulls."

"I'll see what I can do, but the type of face you're talking about is beyond even me. That can only come from Moscow Station."

"Well, keep working on it. And I want a new face for Teresa as well."

"Do you trust her?"

"Not as far as I can throw her, but as long as I can take advantage, I will. If she is working for the other side, she'll choose her moment to betray me, and I'll just have to be careful to watch out for it."

"I hope you know what you're doing, Jack."

"You and me both. But when has that ever stopped me?"

Thorn chuckled. "Good point. Don't leave without telling me. I'll see what I can do on my end."

The call ended and Teresa cleared her throat behind him. He spun, wondering how long she had been standing there. She had nothing on but a towel and it was draped over her arm, hiding nothing.

"I thought you'd like to join me for a shower."

Jack Jr. registered his vote. His eyes took an elevator ride up from her toes to her ponytail.

Why the hell not?

He pointed a finger at her. "Fine. But we're talking shop the whole time."

She winked. "You talk, I'll listen."

His grin spread and he rushed forward, bending over and grabbing her, lifting her up on his shoulder as she squealed. He carried her into the bathroom, the shower already steaming up the confined space.

If the world were going to end, he was definitely going out with a bang.

Operations Center 3, CIA Headquarters

Langley, Virginia

Leroux cleared his throat. "Umm, Red Sonja, your comms are still active."

There was a muffled "sorry" then the feed went silent as Child grinned, spinning in his chair. "My God, I wish I was a spy."

Tong rolled her eyes at him. "It's not just enough to be a spy. You have to have the looks and the charisma."

"Sounds like someone's got a thing for Jack."

Danny Packman grinned. "Both teams have a thing for Jack."

Tong snickered.

Leroux rose, facing his team, cutting off the chatter about Jack's enviable sex life. "While Jack is momentarily thinking with the other head, he was right about one thing."

"What's that?" asked Tong.

"We should be focusing on the hotels. Have we had any luck gaining access to the Warsaw security footage?"

Child held out a hand, tilting it from left to right. "Some. As you know, all the cameras went dead shortly after he entered the hotel with Teresa, all of our comms went dead just before that. Someone from Warsaw Station managed to get in a few hours ago and insert a tap. We're still pulling files from their archive, but every camera that might show something is just dead footage. It's already been gone through and wiped."

Leroux cursed. It was further evidence that this was a well-planned, well-coordinated op, and on the surface, it appeared to contradict Jack's belief that he wasn't the target. "Okay, let's back up the truck for a second. What have we figured out so far?" He turned to Tong. "Run it down."

She pulled up a timeline on her screen, sending it to the main display. "He arrived at the embassy, cleared security, took two glasses of champagne, rendezvoused with Teresa, giving her one of the glasses. They had a short conversation, then Director Nikitin joined them. Jack used the Palance alias for the first time, drained his glass, then faked his illness. Teresa received permission from her boss to take Jack to the hospital. They left the party and her car was brought around. It was scanned clean, but we have no way of knowing if it was bugged with sensors that would activate a short time after the vehicle started moving. They headed for his hotel and arrived twelve minutes later. Review of the footage showed no indication they were being followed. They got out of the car, entered the hotel, and that's when we lost comms. We spotted a former FSB agent in the lobby. Jack and Teresa boarded the elevator, and that's when we lost our camera feeds. We presume they got off on his floor and entered his room. At the time, we had assumed our breach had been discovered, but our latest thinking is that it was cut to cover up his extraction. About fifteen minutes later, we have satellite footage showing Teresa leaving through the front entrance, getting in her car, and returning to her hotel. Ten minutes later the fire alarm went off and the hotel evacuated. Our access to the security cameras returned forty-two minutes later, by which point we presume Jack had been extracted under the cover of the alarm."

Leroux leaned back, tapping his chin, unconsciously mimicking what he had seen Morrison do on countless occasions. "Let's think about this for a moment. If we were running the Russian op, what would be involved?" He pointed at Child. "Go."

Child's eyes bulged. "Me?"

Leroux gave a curt nod. "What would you do?"

Child shifted uncomfortably then shrugged. "Well, being a tech guy, I'd have some sort of tracker on Teresa, certainly her vehicle. I'd have eyes in the sky, satellite or drone, so there's no chance I'd lose her when she made contact. We're assuming though that they knew she'd make contact at the embassy."

"Well, if you remember when I was debriefing her, she indicated when she arrived in Warsaw, her schedule had been completely filled with meetings, most of them not scheduled by her. The only window she had was just before the embassy gathering or after, so they might not have known her meeting would happen at the event, but they would have been prepared to follow her when she left."

Child leaned forward. "Right, so since she's the primary target, I'd have a team nearby and then a second team strategically located somewhere else in the city to reduce drive time for when I figured out where she was going." His jaw dropped. "Wait." He attacked his keyboard then pulled up the transcript of the conversation that had taken place at the embassy. Child pointed at the text now on the main display. "We're forgetting about this."

Leroux quickly read the highlighted portion and smiled. Jack had told Nikitin what hotel he was at for his staycation. "You're right. Up until a couple of hours ago, we've been entirely focused on the idea that Jack was the target, so we just assumed they already knew where he was staying, but if Teresa was the target, then that changes everything."

Tong folded her arms, leaning back. "So, Nikitin is at the party, sees someone approach Teresa, Jack introduces himself as Jack Palance, Nikitin innocently finds out where Jack is staying, he's probably mic'd up so that information is passed on to one of the surveillance teams, they get in position before Jack and Teresa even arrive, and Bob's your uncle."

Child shook his head. "I still can't believe that Nikitin was there. Can you imagine the director of the CIA being involved in an op?"

Leroux grunted. "I could if she were involved in a plot to assassinate the president and wanted to make sure nothing went wrong."

"But wouldn't that mean he was behind the coup, or certainly involved?"

The door hissed open and Morrison entered. Leroux rose as the chief joined him in the center of the room. "Report."

"We're focusing on Jack's hotel in Warsaw. The thinking is if we can somehow figure out who was involved in the op, then we can track them back to their masters and determine who's truly behind this."

"And what have you come up with?"

"Only conjecture so far, but right now the thinking is Nikitin has to be heavily involved."

"What makes you say that?"

"Jack told him what hotel he was staying at, the only time it was ever mentioned. Nikitin must have passed that on to whatever team abducted Jack."

"You're forgetting the brief on the embassy."

Leroux squinted. "Sir?"

"That's the Russian embassy. That entire event was bugged. They can listen in on any conversation anywhere on the floor. While I agree that Nikitin heard where Jack was staying, it definitely doesn't mean that he's the only one that heard it. I guarantee you someone was listening."

Leroux cursed. "You're right, of course. I forgot that."

"Besides, there's something else that might suggest Nikitin isn't the one you should be focusing on."

Leroux's eyebrows shot up. "Oh?"

"I just got out of a White House briefing. It appears that Nikitin is one of the few remaining agency chiefs in Russia to have not yet declared loyalty to the new regime."

Leroux folded his arms and tapped his chin. "I've been monitoring reports of arrests and loyalty declarations, but wasn't really paying attention for his name because I had just assumed he was involved."

"Exactly. We've all been making a lot of assumptions based upon very few facts. The source who provided us with the video footage before the Russians released it has reported that Nikitin has been dodging calls from the Kremlin, and that arrest orders are about to be issued."

"Holy shit!" exclaimed Child as he spun in his chair. "That kind of changes things, doesn't it?"

Leroux had to admit it changed everything. If Nikitin wasn't involved, then what the hell was he doing in Warsaw?

St. Regis Moscow Nikolskaya Hotel

Moscow, Russia

Sherrie stepped into the lobby of the St. Regis hotel, struggling to convey the confidence she didn't feel, Morrison having given her a secret mission known only to the two of them. Her rendezvous with Teresa had been called off at the last moment, Jack apparently collecting her somehow. It was frustrating having someone so key to what was going on, out of the loop. Leroux already suspected Jack's handler Thorn was feeding him information against orders, but how the hell would they have found out where Teresa was? Only Langley could have known that, and of course, Teresa. If she and Jack were working together, then she could have reached out to him. They were still assuming Jack was on their side, that he wasn't involved, yet things like this continually cast doubts. She refused to believe he was involved, yet could understand why Washington wasn't willing to take the risk of bringing him back into the fold.

How the hell had he found out where the woman who could be key to all of this had been hiding, and why had he forced her to go off comms so Langley wouldn't know where he took her? The latest sitrep from Langley suggested the focus had changed. All along they had assumed Jack was the target, but now the belief was Teresa was the one actually being followed to see who she would contact, then whoever that contact was, was set up as the fall guy.

She pinched the bridge of her nose, dealing with an itch, still growing accustomed to wearing the state-of-the-art face mask she now sported. She had rendezvoused with someone from Moscow Station less than ten minutes ago who had delivered her the mask and new ID so she could roam freely, just in case the authorities had managed to get a shot of her face and she was now part of the manhunt underway in Moscow. The mask was incredibly realistic, and the tech had been employed by CIA officers for decades. They were similar to those used in the Mission Impossible movies, though the machine that produced the masks bore only a passing resemblance to the Hollywood contrivance.

Langley had already determined that the authorities had mostly moved on from the hotel, which was interesting in itself. If the man who had assassinated your president was last seen staying in a hotel room only hours ago, wouldn't you be going over the place with a fine-tooth comb searching for evidence? But the police were gone, at least from the lobby and perimeter. Perhaps there were investigators in the room, but there was certainly no evidence that anyone here was aware of the famous guest.

She headed past the elevators and held her phone up against the security pad. It clicked and she pushed open the door marked Employees Only, strolling down the corridor as she tapped on a tablet computer as if she had been here a hundred times before.

"Third door on your right," instructed Leroux in her ear.

She covered her mouth as if to cough. "And we're sure the room's empty?"

"Negative. We haven't been able to gain access to the cameras."

She suppressed the urge to curse as she held her phone against the pad. The panel clicked and she pushed open the door, nearly pissing her pants as two men turned toward her, one sitting at a chair who appeared to be a tech, the other a man in a suit, twenty years her senior. He opened his mouth to challenge her, but she beat him to the punch.

"What the hell are you two doing in here? I was told this area was off limits."

The older man opened his mouth once again but Sherrie didn't give him a chance to say anything as she jabbed a finger at the younger man. "Stop whatever the hell it is you're doing. You could screw up the system."

His hands jerked away from the keyboard. "I was just doing what I was told."

"Who the hell are you?" the older man finally demanded.

"I'm Natalia Angeloff. I was sent from corporate to retrieve all the footage to hand over to the authorities." She eyed him. "Let me guess, you're the authorities?"

The man grunted. "Agent Galkin, FSB."

She cursed. "Does nobody talk to anybody anymore?" She gestured at the young man. "I assume you know what you're doing."

"Yes, ma'am."

"Then keep doing it. We don't want to waste this man's time. From what I understand, moments could count."

"Yes, ma'am." He returned to working the terminal plugged into the security panel, and Sherrie stepped deeper inside, closing the door behind her, standing beside Galkin, mimicking him by folding her arms then staring at the screen.

"Is it true what they're saying?" she asked, lowering her voice slightly. "That the bastard responsible for assassinating the president was staying at this hotel?"

Galkin grunted. "Apparently so."

"Unbelievable. I don't know how the hell the PR department's going to handle this one."

Leroux updated her with what they had found. "Agent Yuri Galkin, forty-six years old, with the FSB for ten years, prior to that, Russian army from the age of twenty-two."

Sherrie listened to the report, saying nothing as she continued to stare at the screen.

Leroux continued. "Now, this is interesting. It says here he's part of Director Nikitin's personal investigations unit. It's a small group believed to be six to eight agents that are at his beck and call. With what's going on, him being there could be considered unusual."

Sherrie desperately wanted to ask why.

"The question is, is he there on behalf of the new regime, or on behalf of Nikitin, who hasn't declared his loyalty yet?"

Sherrie suppressed her smile, Leroux answering her question with one of his own. Her last briefing on the way here had given her the broad strokes of Langley's latest thinking. Initially, everyone had assumed Nikitin was involved because he had been in Warsaw. But if he were, why hadn't he declared his loyalty to the new leader he helped install? Why were papers being drawn up to have him arrested?

She took a chance. "I'm happy to see the FSB is still on top of things, especially with what I just heard on the radio."

Galkin faced her. "What did you hear?"

She leaned closer, lowering her voice to barely a whisper. "That they're preparing to arrest Director Nikitin for not declaring allegiance to the new president."

Galkin regarded her. "You heard that on the radio?"

Sherrie wagged her phone. "Well, not official radio, if you know what I mean."

Leroux cursed in her ear. "What the hell are you doing?"

Galkin waved a dismissive hand. "Don't believe everything you hear, especially on pirate radio."

"Sorry, I'm just scared, I guess. Nobody seems to really know what's going on, and here I am mixed up with it as part of my job."

"I think a lot of people are waking up today to a different reality," the young tech said, chiming in as he continued to work. "I can't say I'm that surprised. I figured somebody would've killed him long ago. What's shocking is that it was the Americans that did it. What were they thinking?"

Galkin grunted. "Don't believe everything you hear on state media."

Sherrie forced her eyes wide and stared at the man. "So, the FSB doesn't think the Americans did this?"

"I've said too much."

Sherrie ignored the statement. "Does Director Nikitin feel the same?"

Galkin eyed her. "There aren't a lot of young people who know who that is."

"Let's just say I'm well-informed and extremely concerned with the future of this country."

Galkin eyed her. "What are you, some sort of activist?"

"No, Agent Galkin, I'm someone who's concerned about the future, and if things continue to head in the direction they appear to be, we could be at war soon. And if things get out of hand, with a madman in charge, it would be the end of everything for everyone."

The young tech cringed. "Jeez, woman, don't be saying things like that about our new president, especially in front of the FSB. You'll get us all killed."

"I don't think we have anything to worry about, do we? Agent Galkin here is part of Director Nikitin's personal investigations unit, and Director Nikitin believes as he does, that America had nothing to do with the assassination." She pointed at the terminal the tech was working. "And the proof might be in those videos."

Galkin folded his arms and scratched at a day's worth of stubble, the man obviously working straight through the night. "You don't work for the hotel."

This was it. This was the leap. This was what Morrison had instructed her secretly to do should the opportunity present itself. "No, I'm here for the same reason you are."

Galkin pursed his lips. "The new president's orders are to kill American agents on sight," he said, switching to perfect English.

"You follow his orders?"

Galkin grunted. "Not bloody likely." He regarded her. "What do you want?"

"I want a copy of all the videos so that they can be analyzed to find out who put our drugged embassy worker in that hotel room. And I want to meet with Director Nikitin, something you're in the unique position to be able to arrange."

The corners of Galkin's lips curled up slightly. "You've got to have the biggest set of balls of any agent I've ever dealt with. Russian or American."

"I'd show you them, but I'm afraid I'd terrify the kid."

He laughed.

"So, do we have a deal?"

"I'll tell you what, you can have a copy of the footage. The more people that have it, the better. I'm not here on behalf of the government, but on behalf of the FSB. We want to determine the truth." He wagged a finger at her. "But be forewarned, if the truth is that America's behind this, then we will be swearing allegiance and backing him in whatever he decides should be done in response."

"And my meeting with Director Nikitin?"

"You'll come back to headquarters with me. He'll either meet with you or have you shot. Which, I can't promise. But if we're going to do this, we'll have to be quick about it, because my contacts are telling me the same thing your pirate radio is saying. The Kremlin is about to move on the FSB. If there's any hope to save Russia, it happens today, because by tomorrow there won't be anyone left with enough power to challenge the lie."

Operations Center 3, CIA Headquarters

Langley, Virginia

Leroux threw up his hands as he turned his chair toward Tong, who was equally shocked. "What the hell just happened?"

Tong stared at him, wide-eyed. "I have no idea, but she just basically admitted to an FSB agent that she's an American spy."

"She's dead," muttered Child as he spun in his chair. He immediately killed his spin and held up a hand. "I'm sorry, I shouldn't have said that." He tapped the palm rest of his keyboard. "I've been reading up on this guy. He's hardcore. He won't hesitate to kill her."

"Randy's right. I read his file too. The fact that she's still alive tells me there's more going on here than an FSB agent conducting an investigation. He could have arrested her right there on the spot, put her in handcuffs and brought her in, but instead"—Tong tapped her headset—"he just let her plug into the hotel's network. We're already getting the download."

Marc Therrien wasn't so optimistic, interjecting from the back of the room. "You might be reading too much into this. While I agree he's there on behalf of the FSB rather than the Kremlin, he might not have taken Sherrie down simply because he's not sure he can. He's twenty years her senior and they're in a confined space. He might be waiting to get her into a more open area where there are other officers that can help him."

Leroux frowned. Therrien was right. This could all be a ploy to get Sherrie into a position for an easier takedown. He activated his mic. "I don't know why you're doing this, but be careful. Don't give him any indication that you're on comms, that way we can monitor. Also, keep your eyes open. Our thinking is he might be looking to get you into a more open area where there are other assets that can help him take you down."

Sherrie cleared her throat once, acknowledging his message, and he breathed a relieved sigh that she wasn't completely disregarding all of his instructions.

The doors to the operations center hissed open and Morrison entered, glancing at the massive display. "Status?"

Leroux rose, slowly shaking his head as he shrugged. "I don't know what the hell's going on, sir. Sherrie just went off the reservation. She basically admitted to an FSB agent who she was, and has somehow managed to wrangle a meeting with Director Nikitin."

A smile spread as Morrison joined him at the center of the room.

Leroux eyed him. "Why do I get the sense that you know exactly what the hell's going on?"

Morrison chuckled. "It's a flyer, I know, but I directly contacted Officer White and instructed her that should the opportunity present itself, she was to attempt to make contact with FSB Director Nikitin."

"And you didn't tell me, her controller?"

Morrison patted him on the shoulder. "Well, I was coming here to tell you that right now. It never occurred to me that she would get the opportunity so quickly. I was thinking I was going to have to send her to FSB headquarters and shake the gate."

"And what if we're wrong about Nikitin? He could have her shot on sight."

"Son, if we're wrong about Nikitin, there's a very good chance all of us, including Officer White, will be dead soon. If we can't get the truth out before the end of the day, Kalishnik will have an iron grip on that country and its nuclear arsenal. Desperate times."

Leroux sighed. "I know, I know. Desperate measures."

Thorn-Arranged Safe House

Moscow, Russia

Jack smiled slightly, relieved at the latest news report. Teresa's personnel photo was featured prominently beside his, but the image of the accomplice, Sherrie, revealed only her chin. If that was the best the Russians were offering up to the press, it was the best they had, meaning her identity was secure for the moment.

The shower had been fun, a good stress reliever that had relaxed him, allowing him to think straight. It had also allowed Teresa to burn off her pent-up energy and participate constructively in their spit balling session.

"He would take my call," said Teresa.

Jack frowned. "I have no doubt he would, but if you're wrong about him, he'll trace the call and have us arrested. And if we're right, where does it get us? It's not like he can protect us. He's probably going to be arrested any minute now. And if we had him bring us in, we'd be arrested along with him."

"Then we don't ask him to bring us in. We contact him and give him our side of the story. More specifically, your side. He obviously has his suspicions."

Jack chewed his cheek for a moment. They had both come to the same conclusion that Nikitin was on the side of truth and the more of that truth he had, the better. But there was another reason to contact him. Nikitin was his way back into the fight. If Washington was going to force Langley to leave him on the sidelines, temporarily becoming a Russian asset might be the only way to clear his name, and proving his innocence might be the only thing that could prevent inevitable war.

He sighed. "Make the call."

Director Nikitin's Office, FSB Headquarters

Moscow, Russia

"We're lucky he's so afraid of you, sir."

Nikitin grunted at his underling's remark. "Is it fear or prudence? He knows he can't send his men here to arrest me. They'd never get past the gates. Arrive with proper paperwork, and that's a different story."

"True. But it buys us some time."

"Time for what? We're no further along in our investigation than we were last night." Nikitin cursed as he tossed his glasses on the desk, rubbing at his tired eyes. "Every minute that goes by, Kalishnik consolidates power. We're the last major holdout, and half my men are itching to join him." He threw his hands in the air. "Who the hell authorized Agent Novikov's identity released to the press? I ordered her released and put under surveillance not only to protect her, but to see what she did and who tried to contact her."

"One of the team must have betrayed us. Or all of them."

"It doesn't matter now, it's too late."

"And you're still convinced she's not involved?"

"No, I think she's a patsy in this. We suspected she was working for the other side, and should we make it through this alive, she'll be going to prison as a traitor. But right now, I don't care about her passing on trivial information to the Americans because of her political beliefs." He paused for a moment as a thought occurred to him. "The initial brief I read on her a few months ago, that'll be eyes only. Almost no one would have access to it."

"True." The man's chin dropped then he smiled. "So, how would they have found out about her to use her?"

"Check the file. I want to know everybody who's seen it, everyone who contributed to it."

"I'm on it, sir." The man spun on his heel and left the office just as the phone buzzed.

Nikitin pressed the intercom button. "What is it?"

Katarina's surprise-filled voice replied. "Sir, I've got Agent Teresa Novikov on the line for you."

His eyes shot wide. "Put her through and trace it."

"Yes, sir."

The line clicked. "Agent Novikov?"

"Sir, thank you for taking my call."

"How could I not? When one of Russia's most wanted criminals calls you, you take it."

"I suppose you do, sir. Sir, I have a confession to make, and depending on what happens over the coming days, it will mean either my imprisonment or death. But my life is no longer important. What is important is the truth, because if your investigation is focusing on me and my contact within the American government, you're wasting time, and those truly behind this are going to get away with it."

Nikitin leaned forward, grabbing a pencil, preparing to take notes. "We don't have a lot of time. Kalishnik's forces will be moving against me shortly. Just give me the complete truth. Don't hold anything back."

"Yes, sir."

And she did. Her story matched everything they had discovered so far. She admitted to passing secrets onto the Americans for several years now, all through a man she had met in Warsaw who worked for the American Embassy, the Jack Palance character he had met only two nights ago. She gave him details without prompting that sealed her fate should that be his goal, but it wasn't. He was attempting to save his country and potentially the world from the madness that now gripped it.

"Why were you in Warsaw?"

"To meet Jack."

"I realize that, but what prompted it this time? Your pattern was always to meet in Moscow."

"The intel I received accidentally was too important and, I felt, too dangerous. I wanted extraction."

"And just what was this intel?"

"It was a report that indicated intercepts suggested the Americans were going to assassinate the president. I knew it was nonsense and that they were going to be set up, which is why I felt they needed to know immediately."

"And how did you come by this intelligence?"

"It was accidentally on the bottom of a pile of files delivered to my office."

"Rather convenient, don't you think?"

She chuckled. "Yes, sir. That's the conclusion we've now come to."

"We?"

"I'm here with Jack."

He bristled. "Wait a minute. How the hell's that possible?"

"Let me explain, sir. The Americans sent an agent to get me out. The person that's now on the news where you can barely see her face. She managed to get me out of my apartment but she came under surveillance. Someone Jack had made contact with after he escaped the hotel reached out to him and told him where I was waiting. He came and picked me up. He's innocent, sir. I swear it."

"Forgive me if I don't take your word for it."

"I understand, sir, and I'd feel the same if I were in your position."

Nikitin stared out the window. "Why are you calling?"

"Like I said, just to make sure that you're not wasting your time on us. From what we're hearing, the Kremlin could be moving on you soon, and we want to help get the truth out there, whatever that truth might be. But in order to help, we need some questions answered."

The door opened and Katarina poked her head inside, shaking her head, indicating the trace had failed. He acknowledged her and she closed the door. "Ask your questions, but I don't promise I'll answer."

"Of course, sir. I guess the biggest question is, why were you in Warsaw?"

It was a fair question, and since he would likely be dead before the day was out, he didn't see any harm in answering it. "We had come across intel that suggested someone was planning to assassinate the president. Certain hardline elements."

"General Kalishnik?"

"No, his name didn't come up specifically, however, people close to him did. We began monitoring their activity and that of their associates, and when you requested temporary duty in Warsaw and it was approved, within minutes, several of those under our watch also booked tickets to Warsaw. Further investigation indicated a team of at least a dozen was dispatched on civilian flights. That was simply too big a coincidence. We already suspected you were a double agent, and it was obvious you were heading to Warsaw to meet with your handler. The question was why was such a large team being sent after you? Because I didn't know when or with whom you'd be meeting, I had your schedule booked solid so that your first possible hand-off would be at the embassy. When your friend faked his illness and you immediately offered to take him to the hospital, it was quite clear he was the contact and the exchange was about to be made. My team monitored to see what happened next, but unfortunately, we had to observe passively, because any of the usual interventions might have been discovered by those we were after. They had jammed all frequencies within the hotel the moment you arrived, and shut down the security cameras, so there was nothing to tap."

"Did you get anything?"

"We have some footage showing a four-man team leaving the rear of the hotel ten minutes after you were spotted leaving, pushing a large box that was then loaded in the back of a truck. It's our belief that your contact was inside that box. We tracked the truck to a private air terminal. It was loaded on a private jet and flown to Ostafyevo Airport just outside of Moscow. Unfortunately, by the time we were able to track where it had arrived, they were long gone, and all the cameras at the airport and in the vicinity of it had been taken down for maintenance for the brief window it would have taken them to unload and transport him out of there."

"They were able to take down security and traffic cameras?"

"Yes. And it was a maintenance shutdown, not a hack. A completely legitimate authorized shutdown."

"By whom?"

"Deputy Director Agapov."

"And is he suspected to be involved?"

"We didn't suspect him at the time, however, Deputy Director Agapov is now Director Agapov, his promotion most likely a reward for his participation."

"We need to get this information out there, sir."

"What information? All we have is four men pushing a box, loading it into the back of a truck. Even if we identified the four of them for who they are, there's no proof of what they were involved in, merely that Russian government assets were on the ground in Warsaw, which isn't unusual. The arrival in Moscow with the shutdown of the cameras will be claimed as routine and merely coincidental. And even if somebody wanted to read something into it, the Kremlin could claim it was a national security matter and obviously had nothing to do with the murder of the president, because an American did it."

"An American staying at that same hotel who went missing at the same time."

"True, but again, all circumstantial."

"Sir, there is a way we can get more information."

"What's that?"

"You have to give what you know to the Americans. We both know their satellite coverage is far better than ours. They might have footage of the airport and the plane arriving, what vehicle Jack was loaded into, where it went."

"If I'm caught cooperating with the Americans, it will discredit anything I might say."

"Sir, let's be frank. If you don't cooperate with the Americans, you'll be dead in the next few hours."

He exhaled slowly, his lips pressed tightly together. She was right. This was no longer a matter of countries. It wasn't Russia against America. This was Old Russia versus New Russia, a new Russia that couldn't be allowed to take hold. And even though America was the enemy of the Old Russia, the old adage remained true—the enemy of my enemy is my friend.

And right now, the real enemy of both America and the Old Russia was General Kalishnik and his forces.

"You're right," he finally said. He closed his eyes. This would certainly seal his fate and that of his family. He opened his eyes and picked up a framed photo of his family, everyone so happy.

I'm doing this for them.

He opened a file on his desk. "I'll give you the flight number, and the departure and arrival times. Tell your American friends I'm running out of time."

"Yes, sir. Thank you, sir. You're doing the right thing."

He frowned.

Then why does it feel so wrong?

Operations Center 3, CIA Headquarters

Langley, Virginia

Leroux stared at the archive footage from a satellite that had a good shot of Ostafyevo Airport at the time in question. The plane taxied to a private hangar and a dozen people disembarked then a crate was unloaded. It was placed in the back of a black van with heavily tinted windows, then it, along with three SUVs, rapidly departed, bypassing all customs and security.

"Interesting," observed Tong. "I didn't see any airport staff anywhere near that."

"Neither did I," agreed Leroux. "So, who has the power to override customs at a Russian airport?"

"Definitely one of General Kalishnik's men would."

"Exactly." He glanced over his shoulder at Child. "Fast forward this. Let's see where they ended up."

"On it."

Morrison entered the operations center and Leroux rose as his boss joined him. "What am I looking at?"

"If we're to believe Director Nikitin, then we believe these are the people who kidnapped Jack."

"Do we have eyes on him?"

"Negative, though we have a crate that matches the one caught on video in Warsaw being loaded into the back of that van, so we believe he's inside."

"Any indication as to where he's going yet?"

"Not yet, sir," replied Child. "But they're using the ring road around Moscow as opposed to going into the city. We should know very soon."

Everyone watched as Child manipulated the satellite image, handing off to a second satellite when the first went out of range. A final flourish at the keyboard and he leaned back, spinning his chair in triumph. "Got it."

Leroux stared at the screen. "Where is that?"

"It's a Russian Army base at Mosrentgen, just on the outskirts of Moscow."

"And under the direct command of General Kalishnik," added Tong.

Leroux turned to Morrison. "Enough of a smoking gun to get Jack off the hook?"

"No. As far as I'm concerned, he was never on the hook, but this won't be enough for Washington. For all we know, this could have been all part of his plan, working together with a rogue element in the Russian government."

"There's one way to know, sir."

Morrison eyed him. "How?"

"His watch."

"What about it?"

"As you know, it has GPS tracking and biometrics. It's been shielded since we lost him at the hotel, and then once he was disavowed, we've been restricted from accessing it. If Internal Investigations could give us access—"

Morrison dismissed the idea. "I've already been briefed. The watch isn't transmitting. It's dead."

"Could it have been confiscated by the Russians and it's still shielded?" suggested Tong.

"Definitely possible."

"Well, there's one way to find out."

Morrison turned to Child. "And what's that?"

"Ask him."

Leroux shrugged. "Why not?"

Morrison pursed his lips, thinking for a moment. "Fine. Ask her to ask him. No direct contact."

Leroux activated his comms. "Red Sonja, Control. Come in, over."

"This is Red Sonja."

"Ask Jack if he still has his Rolex."

"What?"

"You heard me. Ask Jack if he still has his Rolex."

She relayed the question and Jack replied in the background. "Yeah, but it's broken. It looks like it got smashed somehow."

"Did you hear that?"

"Yes. Tell him to extract the flash memory card and transmit it to his handler. And tell him to be careful. It might be the key to everything."

FSB Headquarters

Moscow, Russia

Sherrie's heart hammered as they were waved through the makeshift gates, the guard heavy. The streets surrounding the imposing building were blocked off with dump trucks, FSB personnel scrambling to erect barriers to impede what was to come. There were thousands of people in this complex, but they would be no match if the army showed up with armor.

Galkin glanced at her. "Are you all right?"

"I'm pissing my pants. I never thought I'd ever be here willingly."

He chuckled. "Yeah, I suppose it'd be like me arriving at Langley."

She dismissed the comparison. "Not in the slightest. We don't torture people."

Galkin laughed. "You believe that?"

She smirked. "Well, we don't torture people at Langley."

"Ha. All right, that I believe. Now, we're going to pull up to that entrance over there." He pointed with a finger raised from the steering wheel. "Then we're both going to get out. You're going to follow me inside, walking beside me as if you're my equal. You're going to say nothing. If anyone asks you anything, you don't say a word. Nothing. Not even hello, not yes, not no. You don't nod. You don't blink. I respond to everything. Understood?"

"Yes. But what if they separate us?"

"If they do, then none of it matters. You'll be tortured and eventually killed."

"What would you suggest?"

"Tell them the truth. It worked on me. Who knows? But right now, everybody looks to be on edge, but they're still calm. They know who I am. They know I'm part of the inner circle. The chances of them challenging me are slim."

He pulled up to the entrance and put the car in park. He climbed out and so did she, the keys handed over to a guard, the vehicle already pulling away as they mounted the steps into a building with a terrifying history. A uniformed guard saluted and opened the doors for them. They both stepped into the lobby side-by-side.

Galkin flashed his ID at one of the security personnel. "She's with me. No questions."

The guard snapped out a curt nod as his heels clicked, and they continued toward a bank of elevators nearby. They boarded an elevator and Galkin jabbed the button for the fourth floor then held out his hand, blocking two men in suits. "Take the next one." It was said with such a firm, gruff tone, that both men's eyes bulged and they took an involuntary step back, saying nothing as the doors closed.

Sherrie drew a deep breath, slowly holding it then exhaling, repeating the process as she battled to calm her nerves. Galkin said nothing. They were on camera now. She had to stay in character. They both had to. If anyone suspected anything, they could be greeted by half a dozen assault rifles when the doors opened. The pounding in her ears slowly settled and a bell chimed before the doors opened. She followed Galkin out and they were greeted by four uniformed officers carrying AK-74 assault rifles. Galkin held up his ID again. "She's with me, classified asset, here to meet with the director."

This time his ID was closely inspected. "I'm going to need to see her ID."

Galkin firmly shook his head. "Negative. She's a classified asset. If you become aware of who she is, you'll be terminated."

Nervous glances were exchanged among the guards.

Galkin stepped aside, waving a hand toward her. "Search her. Only her identity is confidential."

Two of the guards eagerly stepped forward, anxious to get their hands on her.

Galkin jabbed a finger at them. "Respectfully search her."

"Yes, sir," they both replied, Galkin's warning immediately changing the nature of the groping hands that were run over her assets, the men forced to be satisfied with feeling her body but not feeling her up, fun bags pressed on rather than treated as squeeze toys. The thorough but respectful search was quickly completed.

"Satisfied?"

Both men nodded, the guard in charge posing one final question, almost hesitatingly. "Sir, with your permission, I'll clear this with the director."

Galkin flicked his hand. "As I would expect you to."

"Thank you, sir."

The man stepped away, picking up a phone on the nearby desk, a whispered conversation taking place before he hung up. "Sorry for the delay, Agent, you're cleared, as is your guest. Director Nikitin is expecting you."

Galkin said nothing, instead heading down the corridor. Sherrie increased the length of her stride to catch up. They stepped through a door into the outer office of Director Nikitin, a gorgeous blonde sitting behind a desk to the left pointing toward the inner office door. "Go ahead, Agent Galkin, he's expecting you."

Galkin opened the door then stepped inside and Sherrie followed. Director Nikitin, a man she would recognize anywhere, sat behind an ornate desk, appearing tired and troubled, and understandably so. He likely wouldn't survive the day if things continued to go the way they were. He stared at her, expressionless.

"Sorry to disturb you, sir," said Galkin. "But I thought it was important you meet this woman as quickly as possible."

Nikitin eyed her. "And you are?"

"A friend," she said in English.

Nikitin smiled slightly. "An American friend?"

"Yes."

"CIA?"

"Who I'm working with or for is irrelevant, and it's best for all of us if I maintain my anonymity. But in any communications with the Americans, you can refer to me as Skylark."

"You have big brass ones, as the Americans might say, to come into my office of all offices of all days."

"Sir, both our countries are about to go to war, and the excuse that's being used is a lie. You know it and I know it. Unfortunately for you, the assets available to you to investigate are rapidly dwindling, and if the truth doesn't get out soon, you'll be arrested and likely executed before nightfall."

"Something I thought would be celebrated at Langley."

"Sir, the man who tasked me to make contact with you said you're a worthy opponent and an honorable one. While we may do things differently, we do our jobs and we're good at them, no matter who we serve."

"And who is this man who tasked you?"

"National Clandestine Service Chief Leif Morrison."

A smile spread and Nikitin leaned back, indicating for them to both sit. "Leif. I've met him on many occasions. I've always enjoyed our conversations. Very sharp and not a diplomat. I can't stand diplomats. They never tell you what they're truly thinking. Leif never lets you not know how he truly feels. I respect that, I respect him, but what proof do I have that he's the one who sent you?"

She shifted in her chair. "This is going to sound odd, and even I don't understand it, but he said you would."

"And what is that?"

"What do you call a fish with no eyes?"

Nikitin tossed his head back and roared with laughter. Sherrie exchanged a puzzled look with Galkin, who shrugged. Nikitin leaned forward and took a drink from a glass of water sitting on his desk, his face slightly red.

"All right, Leif definitely sent you. Now, why are you here?"

"To act as a liaison between you and the Agency. Anything you need, any piece of intel, any camera, any satellite, we can provide it to you. We need to expedite this investigation. And then when you're satisfied we have enough proof to show that not only was the American known as Jack Palance not involved, and we can point to exactly who was, perhaps we can avert a war. But we have to act quickly."

Nikitin regarded her and she wasn't sure what to make of his expression. He was right. If this were any other day, under any other circumstances, she'd be in handcuffs, being taken to the basement, never to be seen again. But this was a day like no other. He needed them and they needed him. The evidence had to come from a respected Russian. It couldn't come from the American side. Washington releasing any proof they might find without a respected Russian voice behind it would be a waste.

Nikitin exhaled. "Very well. I'm dead before the end of the day, regardless. Tell your people that for the moment, the FSB and the CIA are allies."

Thorn-Arranged Safe House

Moscow, Russia

Jack carefully disassembled his broken watch using the tools from his Swiss Army knife that he always had on him. It had been a gift from his parents on his twelfth birthday, his name engraved on it, the surname scratched off in a fit of rage shortly after his parents' death. It was an action he regretted to this day, though there was nothing he could do about it. It was part of who he was. He gently removed the flash memory and inspected it for damage.

"Is it intact?" asked Teresa.

"Yes, it looks like it survived." He launched a custom CIA-designed app that Thorn had forwarded him and placed the chip on the screen. He activated the reader and it immediately began pulling the data off the tiny device using the phone's RFID capability. It was slow compared to other technologies, but it was more secure. Soon Thorn would have all the data from his watch and it would be forwarded to Langley for decryption, then they would finally have some answers. Hopefully enough that would get him back officially on the side of good.

"How long is that going to take?" asked Teresa.

He shrugged, glancing at the progress bar. "Longer than I would've thought. There must be quite a bit of data here."

"More than usual?"

Another shrug. "No idea. I've never actually done this before outside of training."

Teresa halted her nervous pacing in front of the window. "What do we do now?"

"We wait. This will be uploaded in a few minutes. My handler will pass it on to Langley. They'll analyze it, see what jackasses they've been, I'll be reactivated, and then hopefully be given a target to acquire."

She tapped her ear. "They heard that."

"They were meant to." He closed his eyes, the burn indicating how tired he was. He yawned and stretched, exhausted.

She jerked her chin at his phone, still slowly transferring the data. "Do you need to do anything when it's done?"

"No."

"Then how about we go to bed?"

He eyed her. "Am I really so irresistible?"

She laughed. "No. Go to bed to sleep. No hanky panky."

He pushed on his knees and stood. She'd get no argument. He headed into the bedroom and dropped face-first on the rather uncomfortable bed. It shook as she climbed in beside him. He moaned as she removed his shoes, then rolled over to present himself. She tugged at his belt and swatted him.

"I'm just making you comfortable, not starting something." She pulled off his pants then snuggled up beside him. He wrapped his arms around her, and as he drifted off to sleep, far more exhausted than he had realized, images of the assassination threatened to keep him awake.

Thankfully, blissful sleep soon overtook him.

Operations Center 3, CIA Headquarters

Langley, Virginia

"They're both sleeping like babies," laughed Child as he cocked an ear, listening to the overhead speakers. "I think I preferred the animal kingdom from earlier."

Tong rolled her eyes. "You would."

Child shrugged. "Hey, I'm happy and horny. What can I say?"

Therrien was first to deliver the required jab. "I say you put the video game controller down and go out on a Friday night and get laid."

The entire room erupted in laughter at Therrien's insult. Child's cheeks flushed and Leroux had to wonder if the young man was still a virgin. There wasn't any shame in it. He had been a late bloomer himself, and the few unsatisfying encounters he had before meeting Sherrie, in retrospect, weren't worth it. He decided he had to save the young man. "Okay, that's enough. I don't want to have to lose you people to another HR seminar on inappropriate workplace conversations."

Child was already delivering double birds at Therrien. "Don't make me pull your calendar up."

Therrien's eyes narrowed. "What the hell are you talking about, manchild?"

Child shrugged. "Okay, you asked for it." He turned and tapped at his workstation, and a moment later a page from Therrien's shared calendar appeared on the main display. Therrien cursed, immediately recognizing the trouble he had just created for himself. Leroux stared at the image, confused, before finally reading what Therrien had scheduled for Christmas Day only a couple of short months ago.

The room roared.

6:00—Wake up

6:10—Make love to wife

6:20—Open gifts

Tong faced Therrien. "Only ten minutes? Does that include foreplay?"

Therrien attacked his station, desperately attempting to clear the calendar off the screen. It was everything Leroux could do not to laugh. Therrien was notorious for scheduling almost every minute of his day, and this was clearly part of his personal calendar that was never supposed to have been included in the shared one. He snapped his fingers at Child. "Take it down."

"Hey, he started it."

"Yeah, and you definitely finished it. Now take it down."

"Fine." A few taps of the keyboard and the erroneously-shared calendar disappeared.

Therrien sat in the back of the room, humiliated, snickers surrounding him, and Leroux tossed him a bone.

"Okay, everybody forget what they just saw. And for all you guys who can't satisfy your woman in ten minutes, you're doing it wrong."

Therrien shot to his feet, holding his hands out toward Leroux. "Thank you. Sherrie's a lucky woman."

Leroux laughed. "Okay, we're done. Everybody back to work." He caught a glimpse of Tong staring at him a little too wistfully, as if imagining what those ten minutes with him would be like. The woman had a crush on him, had for some time, and they had confronted their feelings for each other. Nothing could happen between them because of his relationship with Sherrie. She had refused his offer of a transfer, instead preferring to remain on the team, promising to work through her feelings and not let them interfere with the job, but it was proving difficult for her and for him. Once he realized her feelings, he discovered he too had a soft spot for her, something he could never act on because he loved Sherrie with all his heart and couldn't imagine life without her.

He ignored the look and returned his attention to his workstation. It beeped with a message from Thorn and the attached data from Jack's watch. He held up a hand, silencing the room. "Okay, we've got the data from Jack's watch. I'm putting it in the shared op folder now. Sonya, you hand out the assignments. I want a team working on the Warsaw timeframe, a team on the Moscow Hotel post wake-up, and another team on what happened in between."

"I'm on it."

Leroux copied the file then began his own analysis. His eyebrows shot up at a large compressed file, something that normally wouldn't be there. He opened it to find a series of image files. He opened the first one and his jaw dropped as he cursed.

It was a copy of the intel that had triggered this entire thing.

Thorn-Arranged Safe House

Moscow, Russia

Jack woke to find junior at full alert, the poor guy confused to find the stump used to transport him from bed to bed was half naked with a gorgeous woman pressed up against him.

"Somebody is happy I'm here," said Teresa, reaching down and making her presence felt.

Jack groaned. "I'm sure I just need to pee." He tapped on her ear. "Any word?"

She held up the tiny device. "They would like to speak with you."

A grin spread. There was only one reason they would want him back on comms. He rolled out of bed and headed for the bathroom as he fit the device in his ear. He activated it as he performed acrobatics in an attempt to relieve himself while otherwise compromised.

"Control, Jackrabbit. Do you read, over?"

Leroux's voice, like that of an angel, replied immediately. "Jackrabbit, this is Control Actual. We read you. Status?"

He stared down at an uncooperative junior. "Debating on whether or not to do a handstand."

"I don't follow you."

"Morning wood, my man, morning wood."

Leroux laughed. "I hear you. You'll be happy to know, despite your enviable erectile difficulties, you've been reactivated."

Jack smiled. "Good. First, I'd like to say it's about damn time. And second, you make sure the official record puts that erectile difficulty comment in context. I've got a reputation to protect."

"I'm sure your reputation is secure. Would you like to know why you're back in the fold?"

"I've been out of it for less than two days and the world's almost gone to hell, so someone decided it couldn't be just coincidence?"

"How'd you guess?"

Jack grinned then groaned as the distraction of the conversation bored junior and he was finally able to do his business. Cheers erupted in the background and Jack shook his head. "Am I on vox?"

"Yep."

"Well, enjoy it while you can, because it won't be in the audiobook version. Now, what did you find? What was I doing?"

"Oh, you're going to love this. You were taken from Warsaw to Ostafyevo Airport, as we recently found out. You were then taken to an army base in Mosrentgen."

"You're not telling me anything new. What *new* did you find out?"

"Wait for it. I rehearsed this."

"I'll make sure the awards shows are notified."

"Thank you. Now this is where it gets interesting, and this is all new information. According to the GPS tracker on your watch, it remained on your wrist and at the base until approximately nine PM yesterday. Biometrics then indicated it was put on someone else's wrist and then it was exposed to what we believe was an electromagnetic pulse that fried its circuitry. The flash memory's protected so it survived, but we have no further tracking from that point on."

Jack cursed. "Well, that's not all that helpful now, is it? Either they knew what the watch was capable of or they just weren't taking any risks that it might have a tracker. So, we still don't know what happened after nine last night."

"No, but you remember from your training what happens when you take that watch off without the proper deactivation sequence?"

Jack smirked. "It begins recording everything."

"Exactly."

"You got something on audio?"

"We did. Listen to this."

There was a hissing sound as the recording began.

"Are you ready?"

"Yes, General."

"Good. It's essential that you succeed. The future of our country depends on it."

"You can count on me, sir."

"I know I can. Now, let's make sure you've got no bugs on you."

Another voice joined in from the background. *"If you'll follow me, Major, this will only take a minute."*

"Won't the EMP fry these glasses?" asked the major.

"Yes, sir, it will. I'll take them."

A door closed and all he could hear was the major's breathing as a whine built up in the background before a slamming sound.

"That ended the recording," said Leroux.

Jack sat on the couch, Teresa eyeballing him, desperate to know what was going on.

"Please tell me you were able to identify those voices."

"General Kalishnik was easy. We have a 98.7% match. It's definitely him."

"And this major?"

"We just got a match on him as well. His name is Major Aleksie Lukin. He was former Spetsnaz until he retired two years ago. That's how we have his voice. After he retired, he became one of Kalishnik's personal bodyguards, so he was naturally watched at any functions he appeared at with the general. We caught him on mic on several occasions so put him in the database because of who he was. As soon as we told the computer that we were looking for a Russian major, it spit him out within minutes."

"So, we have the voice of the assassin talking with the general about the assassination at the Mosrentgen army base?"

"Yes, though the references to the actual assassination are tangential at best."

Jack sighed. "Do we know where he is now?"

"We have him on camera with General Kalishnik at the Kremlin."

"We need to get our hands on him."

"To what end? I doubt he's going to admit to what he did."

Jack pressed a hand gingerly against his side. "You're forgetting one thing."

"What's that?"

"I have injuries. They would've been made after the fact, not before, so that they matched up with anything caught on video."

Teresa's eyes shot wide. "So, he'll have matching injuries."

"Exactly." He gasped at a sudden realization.

"What's wrong?" asked Teresa, Leroux echoing the same concern.

"I just figured out how they did it."

Operations Center 3, CIA Headquarters

Langley, Virginia

Leroux leaned back in his chair, stunned at Jack's explanation. It made perfect sense and it fit all the facts. The entire time, the only doubts he had about Jack's innocence were triggered by his memory of the event. How could he possibly have memories of the deed if he hadn't actually done it?

Tong turned in her chair to face him. "It's brilliant."

"Oh, yeah. I guarantee you we're going to be using it at some point as well."

"So, you think this completely clears me?" asked Jack.

"I'm guessing it does for any of those who had doubts, but right now it doesn't really help us that much with the Russians. It just answers the biggest damn question that's been hanging over this the entire time. How the hell did you remember doing something you couldn't have possibly done? The tape proves that the glasses have electronics, and the video of the event shows that the major was wearing glasses the entire time. Obviously they have a camera in them and recorded everything from his perspective, and then when everything was said and done, that video was played over and over for you to watch while you were still in a drugged state."

"It was driving me nuts. I knew there was something wrong with the memory. It just didn't feel right. It wasn't until the reference to the glasses being removed before the EMP that everything clicked. They were obviously replaying the video in front of me, and I was watching it, but every time he moved his head, mine wasn't moving. That's what was wrong. In a real memory, a real dream, your head is moving with the perspective that you're witnessing. In this case it wasn't, so it was like watching someone playing a video game and my brain just couldn't figure it out." Jack laughed. "Thank God. For a while there, I wasn't sure if I was actually innocent."

"Well, I never really doubted you."

Child grinned. "I was convinced he was guilty the entire time. Happy to know I was wrong."

Jack laughed. "Deliver a bird for me, would you?"

Leroux did as told. "That's from Jack."

Child bowed. "Well deserved."

"I still think we need to get our hands on the major," said Jack. "Find him for me and tell Moscow Station that we need faces and IDs ASAP."

"Consider it done. There's one more thing you need to be made aware of."

"What's that?"

"Sherrie is with Director Nikitin. She's now the liaison between the FSB and the CIA."

Jack cursed. "Is she insane? Whose moronic idea was that, because it certainly wasn't hers. She's too smart for that."

Child snickered. "Good thing the Chief's not here."

Morrison's voice cut in over the speakers, Leroux fully aware based on the indicator on his screen that the Chief was listening in from his secure office. "It was my idea."

Jack groaned. "Somebody could have warned me."

Leroux cleared his throat. "Well, I didn't think it was actually necessary. Normally, you're not stupid enough to mouth off about the brass."

"Sorry, Chief. I'm sure you had a brilliant reason for handing one of our officers over to the FSB."

"I did. The enemy of my enemy is my friend."

Jack grunted. "Everybody always quotes Sun Tzu, but did the man actually ever win a battle?"

Leroux's eyebrows rose slightly at the interesting question that had never occurred to him to ask.

Jack continued. "Does his little Art of War book make any mention of what happens when your new ally is killed by your mutual enemy and you're left standing alone in his tent? The moment they make their move on Nikitin, Sherrie is as good as dead."

Leroux cringed at the thought he had been attempting to stifle the entire time.

"I'm well aware of that," said Morrison. "Which is why we need to act swiftly. I'm working on an inside contact to see if we can get access to the raw camera footage from the incident. What was released were selective angles where you couldn't see the face until the very end, and that was too zoomed in. Jack's face was isolated so you couldn't see any of the background, and it was only for a few frames. They probably got that while they had him in captivity. Chris, get Jack everything he needs from Moscow Station. The Pentagon has just briefed the president that a large group of Russian regulars are marshaling for a move on FSB headquarters. This could all be going down in about an hour."

Leroux closed his eyes for a moment, inhaling deeply. "Understood, sir. We're on it."

"God help us if we fail," muttered Child.

Director Nikitin's Office, FSB Headquarters

Moscow, Russia

Sherrie watched as Nikitin's face turned red with rage as he listened to the audio recording just received from Langley. He jabbed a finger at Agent Galkin. "Get a copy of that to our people. I want the voiceprint IDs confirmed and then I want every video archive we have access to gone through. Somebody had to see him at the Kremlin last night."

Galkin handed her his card. "Email the file to me."

She did as told and Galkin confirmed he had it on his phone then left, leaving her alone with a man she still dreaded. The FSB had no morals. It wasn't a respectable spy agency, the actions of its agents often brutal and far too often illegal under international law. It was a reflection of the man who ran it, a man who could change his mind about her status here in a heartbeat.

Nikitin's phone rang and he picked it up. "Yes?"

There was a pause then he frowned. "Understood. Sound the alert and lock us down." He hung up the phone and a moment later an alarm blared on the other side of the door.

Sherrie tensed. "What's going on?"

"The order for my arrest has been issued. A large contingent of soldiers loyal to General Kalishnik have been dispatched."

"When will they get here?"

"Their rally point is at Mosrentgen where your friend Jack was being held. A column moves slowly, especially through city streets, so we've got about an hour before they arrive."

"Understood." She held her finger up to her ear. "May I inform my people?"

"Yes. And should you wish to leave before they get here, I'll release you from your commitment."

She dismissed the notion. "Unless they order me to leave, I'm staying. If we fail and our two countries go to war, whether I die an hour from now or ten days from now doesn't matter. Dead is dead."

Director Morrison's Office, CIA Headquarters

Langley, Virginia

"Security is tight, Leif, extremely tight. I bought myself a little bit of space by being one of the first to declare my loyalty to the new president. I'm now the Deputy Minister of the Interior."

"Congratulations," replied Morrison. "Let's just hope there's an interior left for you to help manage."

Dimitri Garin grunted. "Let's hope. Listen, I can't get my hands on the footage you need. I've tried, but I'm too visible, and all that footage is in an area of the complex that I have no business being in."

"I've got two people that can get to the video if you can get them inside. Can you?"

"I should be able to. Our new president is trying to make things appear as if it's business as usual, as if there's been an orderly transition of power. Security is heavy, but visitors are being allowed. Get me their details and I'll get them on the list. Are they any good?"

"The best." It was a partial truth. Jack was the best. Teresa, he had no idea, but he couldn't let their only inside man be aware of any doubts.

"Let's hope they are, because if they get caught, I'll be in front of a firing squad before the sun sets."

"Yes, but remember, my friend, if they succeed, this could all be over by sunset."

Thorn-Arranged Safe House

Moscow, Russia

Jack stood in front of the mirror, familiarizing himself with all the honors and insignia on the uniform delivered by Moscow Station. He was now Lieutenant Colonel Leonid Aminoff, high enough a rank that he wouldn't have to deal with the riffraff, but low enough that if no one recognized his face or name, it wouldn't come off as unusual.

Teresa emerged in a lieutenant's uniform. "Lieutenant Petra Lipovsky, personal aide to Lieutenant Colonel Leonid Aminoff, reporting for duty, sir." She snapped out a salute.

Jack faced her. "You've memorized your packet?"

"I think so."

He stared at the unfamiliar face, the freshly printed mask from Moscow Station a woman with plain features, someone who wouldn't draw attention like Teresa might normally. His own mask was unremarkable as well, and they were exact matches for two Russian officers that existed in the database, but Langley indicated were on separate vacations out of the country. Should either of them be challenged as to why they were in Moscow, the answer was simple—the president was dead and it was their duty to return immediately.

"Let's go." Jack tapped his ear. "Langley said Kalishnik's people are moving on the FSB now." He headed for the apartment door. "Just remember, confidence is key. If you believe you should be there, then they'll believe it as well. Appear uncertain or uncomfortable, you're going to stand out like a sore thumb and will be challenged."

"I have done this before."

"Never with stakes this high." He frowned as he opened the door. "I suppose you're right. You'll do fine. Like you said, you've done this before. Just treat this like any other op."

She smirked. "Most of my ops end with me in bed with someone."

He grinned at her. "Lieutenant, if we survive this, this superior officer will be all over you tonight."

She smiled then patted his face as they waited for the elevator. "I hope you'll take that off before you invade my borders. Lieutenant Colonel Aminoff is not an attractive man."

He winked. "There are things we can do where you never see my face."

The doors opened and they boarded the empty elevator.

"Lieutenant Colonel, if we succeed in saving the world, I'm not looking for a shag. I want to be made love to."

He laughed. "One romance package coming up."

She shuddered, staring up at him. "You're really not very attractive right now."

"The colonel does nothing for you?"

"Absolutely nothing."

"Poor guy. I didn't think he was that bad."

"You don't have to sleep with him."

"This is true."

The doors opened and a young couple boarded, ending their conversation. They would be at the Kremlin in less than fifteen minutes, which meant they could be getting the evidence to save the world in another fifteen, or dead on the marble floor in less than that.

Either way, this was ending for them soon.

Operations Center 3, CIA Headquarters

Langley, Virginia

Leroux stood in the center of the room, his hands clasped behind his back as several different satellite feeds were shown on the massive display. They were following a large column slowly winding through the city for almost an hour. Estimates suggested approximately 500 personnel, most in troop transports accompanied by several dozen armored vehicles. Four attack helicopters had just been dispatched from Kubinka Air Base and were en route to rendezvous with the column at FSB headquarters. According to Sherrie, voluntarily remaining at her post, the building was on full lockdown and pretty much everyone now carried a weapon.

It was the old Russia's final stand.

The only hope for peace rested in the hands of a group of people he had always considered his archenemies, and the ability of Jack to acquire the final piece of evidence that would clear his name and prove who was truly behind what had happened last night. He glanced over at the

DEFCON indicator, still on 2, and another shiver ran up and down his spine. It was terrifying to think how close they were to all-out war, all because some men craved power over all else.

Morrison entered the operations center and joined him. "Report."

"The column is less than ten minutes away from the Lubyanka building."

"How long do you think they can hold out?"

Leroux sighed. "If everyone within those walls is on the same side, they could hold out quite a while, but we have to assume at least some of them support the new president. And remember, this is the FSB. For all we know, the majority support the new president."

"And Jack?"

Leroux pointed at the upper right corner of the display, a map shown with a pulsing red dot. "He and Teresa are en route. They'll be arriving at the outer gate in less than two minutes. If they make it through perimeter security, then whoever your contact is did his job. They still have to make it through the secondary checkpoint, then it's all up to Jack. I'm a little concerned about Teresa. She doesn't have the experience."

"So am I," agreed Morrison. "We'll have to trust Jack's judgment on this. In situations like this, two people draw less attention than one. The estimate I read was less than fifteen minutes before we could see data. Is that accurate?"

"Yes, sir. If your contact is correct and General Kalishnik is trying to give the appearance of business as usual inside the walls, then we should be able to assume there aren't all kinds of new checkpoints internally. From the deputy minister's office to the server room is less than a five-minute walk. Once inside, he just needs to insert a tap and we should have full access through a satellite link that they won't be able to detect. I've got two ops centers going, and every single analyst in both will be searching for the correct files. If we're lucky, we'll find what we're looking for within a few minutes. If we're unlucky, it could take half an hour to an hour."

Morrison frowned. "That's a lot of time for them to be discovered."

"I know. I instructed Jack to leave the moment the tap is in place, but he refused. He intends to stay and hold the room to give us as much time as possible."

Morrison cursed. "I hate to say it, but he's right. And besides, even if I were to order him out, he'd fake a comms failure. Do you have our package ready?"

"It's just waiting for the final footage and then it'll be broadcast worldwide and through social media. The critical thing is we need the Russian military made aware of what we find, especially those commanders who declared their loyalty to Kalishnik. My guess is the majority are doing it out of fear as opposed to loyalty. Most sane commanders don't want war, and certainly don't want nuclear war. It'll be going out over all the hotlines established between NATO and Russia, plus Moscow Station over the years has gathered a shitload of phone numbers for senior officers and political leaders. We'll be sending repeated text messages with links, and then we'll have a live feed from Director Nikitin going out along with it, assuming he's still alive. This is all going down in the next hour."

Morrison faced him squarely. "No matter how this goes down, I know you did your best." He turned to the room. "You all did your best. Whatever happens, the credit is all yours, but none of the blame. Should we fail and there's anyone left alive to write the history of this day, no one will lay fault at the feet of anyone in this room."

"Jack's arriving at the gate now," reported Tong, her voice subdued, not wanting to interrupt Morrison.

Morrison smacked his hands together. "This is it, people." He patted Leroux on the back. "It's your show, son." He smirked. "No pressure."

Approaching the Kremlin

Moscow, Russia

"This is it. Now remember, don't worry about appearing a little nervous. Everybody is with what's going on. Just remain in character. You're my aide. I ordered you to return from vacation the moment I heard about the assassination. You did as ordered and now we're here to meet with Deputy Minister Garin for a classified briefing, the details of which you're not privy to. If you're challenged on your loyalties, what's your answer?"

Teresa drew a breath as they approached the gate. "From what I've been told, the Duma has named General Kalishnik as president, therefore my loyalties lie with him."

"Perfect."

Jack pulled up to the gate in the sedan arranged by Moscow Station. They were immediately surrounded by troops, automatic weapons pointed directly at them. A bomb sniffer dog slowly circled the car as mirrors were extended underneath, searching for explosives or any other hidden devices. Jack held out his ID to the guard.

"State your business."

"I'm here to give a briefing to President Kalishnik's new Deputy Minister of the Interior. I was informed I'm on the list."

"Wait here." The guard stepped away and into the security station built into the wall surrounding the massive complex. Jack glanced over at Teresa, who sat quietly beside him. Her jaw was clenched and her breathing was slightly elevated, though nothing noticeable. If anything were to give them away, it was her eyes darting about.

"Security's a lot heavier than when I was here last time," he said in Russian.

She flinched. "Much." She relaxed slightly at his voice.

"Hopefully this won't delay our meeting with the deputy minister. I'm sure he's got enough to worry about with the transition."

"Yes, sir. Hopefully."

The guard returned and handed back the ID. "You're cleared to proceed, Lieutenant Colonel, I'm sorry for the delay."

Jack took the ID back. "No need to apologize for doing your job well, Corporal." He put the car back in gear and pulled through the gates, weaving through several sandbagged positions.

Teresa leaned forward slightly. "This is better."

Jack agreed. Once they were through the throng of security at the gate, everything thinned out, making it appear like any normal day. He pulled into a guest VIP parking lot, then two minutes later they were clearing building security, though things were much more relaxed here, the guards working under the assumption that those outside had already done their jobs properly. They were again verified to be on the list and were cleared.

"Do you know where you're going, sir?"

"Yes. I've been here before many times," replied Jack as he clipped on his visitor badge. "If we get lost, we'll just ask. I'm certain everyone in this building is a friend."

The guard smiled. "Yes, sir. Of that, you can be certain."

"Good to hear it. The last thing we need today is disloyalty to our new duly named president."

"Yes, sir."

Jack headed for the elevators, Teresa at his side and slightly back. They boarded the crowded car then got off on the third floor, exactly as they would be expected to. They were cleared by yet another security detail before entering the outer office of Deputy Minister Garin. The secretary's eyes bulged but she waved them in.

"He's expecting you." Her hand trembled as she pointed to the inner door, as if she were aware of exactly what was going on.

They stepped inside and a man, perhaps late thirties, rose from behind his desk to greet them. "Colonel Aminoff, it's a pleasure to meet you."

Jack reached out and shook the man's hand. "The pleasure is mine, Deputy Minister. My aide, Lieutenant Lipovsky."

Teresa bowed, hanging back by the now-closed door.

"I'm here to provide you with your classified briefing in preparation for your new role."

Garin waved a hand, dismissing the pretense. "The room has been swept. There are no listening devices here. I assume you know where you're going?"

"Yes, sir. Sublevel Two, hang a right out of the elevators, room S204."

"Good, then I won't keep you. I've just received word that troops loyal to General Kalishnik have just arrived at FSB headquarters. Once they fall, all hope is lost." Garin rounded his desk and opened a drawer. "I assume they confiscated your side arms."

"We didn't bother bringing any."

"Wise." He reached into the drawer and pulled out two Makarovs plus two extra mags for each. "I have a feeling you might need these."

Jack smiled and took the weapons, handing one over to Teresa. She inspected it, as he did his before he tucked it behind his back. He took the spare mags and pocketed two of them, handing the other two to Teresa.

Garin passed over a piece of paper on official government letterhead. "Orders for you to inspect the server room on behalf of the interior minister, just in case you're challenged for being in the basement."

Jack took the page and tucked it into the inside breast pocket of his jacket. "Good thinking." He extended a hand and Garin took it.

"Good luck, whoever you are."

Jack smiled. "Good luck to us all. I highly recommend you leave the building and hide out somewhere in case things go wrong. They'll inevitably track things back to you."

Garin rejected the idea. "My place is here. If you succeed, calm voices will be needed to prevent a repeat of what happened overnight."

"You're a brave man, sir."

Garin laughed. "I'm a terrified man, but I love my country and I'll do whatever it takes to steer her in the right direction, no matter how much she resists. Now, get out of here. We're running out of time."

Jack bowed slightly then left Garin's office, Teresa on his heels. He acknowledged the terrified secretary and headed for the elevators. The guards snapped to attention and Jack took a chance. He retrieved the orders Garin had given him and waved it at the lieutenant in charge. "We have orders from the deputy minister to inspect the server room on sublevel two." He jerked his chin at the guard detail. "Can we expect the same reception?"

"Yes, sir. Every floor has heightened security."

Jack frowned. "I thought it was supposed to be business as usual?"

"It is, sir, for the most part. Once you're on the floor and cleared by security, you're good."

Jack let a string of creative Russian curses erupt and handed over the orders. "Read this, satisfy yourself that they're valid, then you'll escort us to the basement and clear us through security. We don't have any time to waste. The assault on FSB headquarters is starting now, and the deputy minister has reason to believe they may have somehow infiltrated the system."

The lieutenant's eyes bulged at the lie. He quickly read the orders and handed them back. "I'm satisfied these are valid, sir." The elevator chimed and the doors opened. Jack stepped on board followed by Teresa. "Let's go, Lieutenant. No time to waste."

The lieutenant hesitated, no doubt given orders not to leave his post.

Jack held out an arm, blocking the doors from closing. "That's an order, Lieutenant, or do you want to be the one responsible for allowing the FSB to sabotage our efforts?"

The young man gulped then turned to his second-in-command. "I'll be right back."

"Yes, sir."

The lieutenant boarded the elevator and Jack hit the button for sublevel two. "If asked, you're not to tell them what the deputy minister suspects. If the FSB has managed to infiltrate our system, then it was most likely done by someone with regular access. That means don't trust anybody normally stationed on sublevel two."

"Yes, sir. I understand, sir."

They rode the rest of the way in silence as Jack urged the elevator on, praying for no stops along the way. They reached the ground level then passed it, and he suppressed the urge to sigh. The doors opened on Sublevel 2 and their escort stepped out.

"This is Lieutenant Colonel Aminoff," said the lieutenant to his counterpart. "He's already cleared security and is here on an urgent matter for the Deputy Minister of the Interior."

Jack stepped out and Teresa stood in the door, holding the elevator. He held up his orders. "Do you need to see these or is the word of your fellow officer enough, Lieutenant?"

The man snapped to attention. "No, sir. The lieutenant and I are well acquainted and I trust him."

"Very good." Jack turned to their escort. "Thank you, Lieutenant. Return to your post."

"Yes, sir."

The lieutenant boarded the elevator that Teresa had held, the buzzer inside silencing once she stepped away. Jack strode with purpose down the corridor, counting off the doors before finally turning his head slightly, spotting the server room. His visitor pass had access to nothing, though his newly acquired CIA-customized phone might, but would draw too much attention. He knocked, three firm raps. The door opened a moment later and a young man with a haircut that would never pass muster in the military opened the door. His eyes widened at the sight.

"Colonel, can I help you, sir?"

Jack pushed him aside and stepped in, the man scrambling backward. "We're here for a surprise inspection by order of the Deputy Minister of the Interior."

"We weren't told."

"Of course you weren't told. If you're the source of the leak, you'd have time to hide your activity." Jack sensed he was about to be challenged and took a step closer. "Are you the source of the leak? Are you the one that betrayed our new president?"

Another involuntary step backward had the fight fleeing the man. "No, sir. I assure you, I'm loyal to the president."

"Then you've got nothing to worry about. How many are in here?"

"Just me and my supervisor."

Jack held out his hand. "Surrender your security pass."

The pass was unclipped from its lanyard and handed over as an uber dork if there ever was one rounded the bank of servers. "What's going on here?"

"Security inspection."

"I wasn't informed."

"Of course you weren't. What's the point of having a surprise inspection if everyone knows it's coming? Why are you people surprised by this?"

"I'm going to have to clear this."

"No, you don't."

"Listen, Colonel, I don't care who you are, but nobody accesses this room without authorization."

"I have orders from the deputy minister for a snap inspection." Jack produced the orders but the new arrival refused to take them.

"Those are *your* orders, Colonel, not mine. I don't fall under the Interior Ministry's chain of command. Now, I am more than willing to cooperate, but I have to clear this with my superiors. If they say it's all right, we'll assist you in whatever way possible."

Jack cursed and took a step forward, grabbing the man by the shirt and hauling him toward him while taking a step to the left. He wrapped his arm around the man's neck then braced it with his other arm, squeezing tight, cutting off the flow of oxygen to the defiant man's brain. Teresa stepped forward, drawing her weapon, and pressed it against the younger one's chest. His arms shot in the air as he surrendered, his terrified eyes watching while his coworker slumped to the ground.

Jack released the now unconscious man and turned. "Your name?"

"P-Pavel."

"All right, Pavel, you're aware of what's happening at FSB headquarters?"

"Yes, sir."

"Then you agree, it's essential our troops succeed?"

"Yes, sir."

"Well, that's why we're here. We have reason to suspect the FSB planted footage on our servers, casting doubt on what happened yesterday. It's our job to find that footage. Can I count on you?"

"Of course, Colonel."

"Good." Jack stepped back and Teresa lowered her weapon. "Show us the way."

Pavel led them deeper into the room to several stations in the back. He took a seat and Jack sat beside him, giving a surreptitious nod to Teresa. She disappeared behind a rack of servers. Jack pulled out his phone and it showed no signal.

"Are we blocked in here?"

Pavel nodded. "It's a Faraday Cage. No signals in or out that aren't hardwired."

Jack eyeballed him. "But you have a way around it, don't you?"

Pavel shifted uncomfortably. "Sir?"

"There's no way two computer geeks like you stay holed up in this room for eight hours a day, without being able to check your messages. Listen, tell me now and I blame the other guy. Don't tell me and I find out how, I blame both of you."

Pavel, trembling, opened a drawer on the workstation and removed a small pyramid-shaped device. He plugged in the power supply then reached behind the workstation, pulling forward a standard network cable. He plugged it in the back of the small device. "I swear I didn't set it up, sir. It's been here for as long as I have been."

"And how long is that?"

"Just over a year."

"How does it work?"

"It's a Wi-Fi to cellular converter. You connect your phone to the hidden network and it transmits everything over the cable, outside of the Faraday Cage, where everything's then transmitted by cellular. "I swear we just use it for social media. It's so damned boring in here, it's the only way we keep sane."

Jack pulled up the Wi-Fi settings on his phone.

"The network is hidden, sir."

Jack handed the phone over and Pavel connected him to the private network before handing it back a moment later. Jack connected successfully to a secure CIA FTP site. "Good, now let's bring up the security footage of the assassin."

"Sir?"

"You heard me."

"That was ordered deleted earlier today."

Jack cursed. "Why the hell would they delete the footage of the man who assassinated our president?"

Pavel shrugged. "I don't know, sir. All I know is somebody came in earlier and ordered us to copy all the footage then delete it."

Teresa rounded the corner and held up her cellphone, shaking her head. Jack swatted Pavel on the shoulder. "Connect her to the private network." He did as told and Teresa disappeared once again behind the racks of servers. "Is there any way to undelete it?"

"No. They had us do an aggressive wipe of the drives."

"All the cameras in the entire facility or just in the president's office?"

"Just his office and the cameras leading to it. They had a specific list of feeds they wanted wiped."

Jack cursed.

"But…"

Jack stared at Pavel. "But what?"

"Well, sir…" Pavel sighed. "I swear this wasn't my idea."

"I don't give a shit whose idea it was."

"Well, sir, our orders were to delete the hard drives, so we did that, but we don't have write access to the backups. They're stored off-site and there's no way for us to delete anything from here. We can access them to restore files, but we can't delete them."

"And did you tell them this?"

"No. We were both too nervous to say anything."

"So, if they haven't had a chance to delete the backups yet, you can still access them?"

"Yes."

Jack snapped his fingers. "Let's do it. Hurry."

Pavel worked the station and moments later, a directory structure appeared on the screen. "They're still here."

"Start pulling all those files down onto this server."

"If anybody's monitoring, they'll know what's happening."

"I don't care. We need those files. The FSB is up to something. In fact, the person who ordered you to delete them might actually be FSB." Jack pointed at the screen. "Put them all into a separate directory. We don't want to actually restore the backups."

"Yes, sir." Pavel got to work, and moments later a progress bar appeared showing the files being restored to a newly created directory. Jack fired a message to Langley with the directory path, and if Teresa had done her job right planting a tap disguised as a makeup case, Langley should have full access.

His secure messenger indicated a reply.

Receiving the files now.

"How long is this going to take?"

"To restore everything? It could be a couple of hours."

"What about just the office?"

"Oh, we'll have that probably in five minutes or so."

Five minutes and the job was done. Even if they didn't make it out of here alive, the mission would be a success.

Somebody pounded on the door.

Operations Center 3, CIA Headquarters

Langley, Virginia

Leroux leaped to his feet as the files poured in. "This is it, people. You know your jobs. Time is of the essence. Once you identify the camera feed as something we need to look at, shout it out and add it to the list. Priorities are the cameras showing the assassination itself, and secondary is anything showing the assassin making entry and escaping."

"I've got the office," announced Tong.

Leroux looked at the first entry in the priority list as one of his analysts announced they were on it. He jumped into the directory himself as the doors to the operations center opened. He glanced up to see Morrison and the director of the entire damn CIA walk in. He made to stand but Morrison waved him off.

"Keep working, everybody."

Leroux did as told, pulling up the first file in the directory that had completed downloading, and smiled. It showed the office with the president sitting at the far end of the room at his desk, the time code showing five minutes before the leaked video took place.

He held up his hand. "The first file in the directory is five minutes behind what we're looking for." He dragged the arrow in the progress indicator and the video raced ahead. It was a different angle than what they had been shown, but it was still from the back. The assassin strode into the room, directly toward the president, and fired six rounds then turned.

"Holy shit!" he cried as he tapped the keyboard and brought the footage up on the main display. "We've got it!"

Everyone watched as the assassin turned, revealing his face, and it was Major Lukin, not Jack.

"Is that the proof we need?" asked Director Gladys McQuay.

Leroux nodded. "It should be. And we should be able to get even more footage as well." He indicated the display. "And look how crisp it is. Those are full 4K security cameras, not the grainy crap that they released to the press to hide the details."

Morrison slapped him on the back. "Then put together the package and get it to Director Nikitin immediately, and get this out for the world to see. We've just received word that the Russians launched their Northern Fleet, armed with nuclear weapons for the first time in thirty years. Minutes count."

"We're on it, sir." Leroux forced a smile. "And things would go quicker if—"

"We got the hell out of here?"

"Your words, sir, not mine."

Director McQuay laughed. "He's right, Leif. Let's let these people do their jobs. We have to inform the president of what's about to happen." She headed for the door, followed by Morrison, and Leroux returned his attention to the job at hand.

A message came through his desktop from Jack.

We're about to lose our position. Have you got what you need?

Leroux's heart raced with the update and he typed a quick reply.

We have footage of the assassin showing his face. More is always better.

The reply was immediate.

No promises. Will hold out as long as we can.

Leroux desperately wanted to order him to surrender, but it would be the wrong call. The more footage they had, the more irrefutable the proof became. Two lives lost to save billions was a small price to pay, yet it sickened him.

He was the one ordering them to their deaths.

Good luck.

Server Room S204, The Kremlin

Moscow, Russia

Jack helped Teresa shove a large filing cabinet in front of the door as the pounding continued. Security passes had been used to unlock the door several times, but Jack had managed to shove it back shut so far. Each time the door opened a sliver, more voices could be heard as additional security personnel gathered. All it would take would be for them to get the door open long enough to toss a grenade in, and this was over.

The door clicked open again then swung in, smacking the filing cabinet, easily shoving it aside. Jack raised his Makarov and fired through the opening, two rounds. His target dropped and he fired again at his next target. Two more to the chest. They had six mags between them and that was it. Their opponents had unlimited firepower. The enemy scurried back and he stepped out, grabbing his first victim by the collar and hauling him through the door before jamming it shut. Teresa shoved the cabinet back in place as he stripped the soldier of his body armor and tossed it to her.

"Put this on."

She refused. "No, you should wear it."

"Put it on!" he ordered. He relieved the corpse of an AK-74 assault rifle plus two mags along with a sidearm and its two magazines. They were better armed now, and judging by the fact that the two he had shot were two of the four originally at the elevator, it suggested a full tactical team hadn't arrived yet. Once they did, this was over.

Everything went abruptly dark and a moment later, battery-operated emergency lights activated, the hum of their power cells vibrating through the room.

Jack cursed. "Pavel, do we have backup power for the servers?"

"Yes, sir."

"You're still downloading?"

"Yes, sir."

"How long will that last?"

"Only a few minutes. The backup power in here is meant to give the diesel generators time to kick in. From what I can see, they've disabled them."

"Two minutes, ten minutes, what?"

"I'd say five minutes."

"Are you needed at that keyboard?"

"No."

Jack jerked his chin at Teresa. "Go tie him up. Make it look like he didn't participate."

She nodded and headed back behind the racks of servers as he made a decision which could change everything.

He was going out with a bang.

Director Nikitin's Office, FSB Headquarters

Moscow, Russia

The entire building shook as an explosion rocked the main entrance. The wrought iron gates whipped across the stone courtyard as scores of Russian troops loyal to General Kalishnik surged through the entrance, the muzzles of their rifles flashing in the dusk. Hundreds of weapons opened up on them from the surrounding buildings and various prepared positions, and the initial wave took heavy casualties.

Sherrie watched it all unfold through the window to Director Nikitin's office. The main power had been cut moments before the assault began, and generators now provided limited power. Nikitin was on his phone, barking orders, when Sherrie spotted a bright flash from beyond the defensive perimeter.

"Get down!" she cried as she dove to the floor, a round from a tank slamming into the building, shattering all the windows. Nikitin continued, unfazed, when Leroux squawked in her ear.

"Skylark, Control, come in, over."

"This is Skylark, go ahead."

"We've got it! Transmitting it to your tablet now. We're sending all the footage we have, all the proof, all the evidence, to every single news organization and government in the world. We're also sending it out over social media."

"It proves it wasn't Jack?"

"Yes. It's Major Lukin as we suspected. I'm sending the video to your tablet now. We need Nikitin on video confirming its authenticity."

"I'm on it." She checked her tablet and saw the file downloading. She waved the device at Nikitin. "We've got it. Are you ready?"

He held up a finger and finished his call before hanging up the phone. "Katarina, get in here!"

His secretary rushed into the room and he pointed at the phone. "Put this on intercom. I want everybody in the building and outside to be able to hear what I have to say."

"Yes, sir."

Sherrie confirmed the file had completed downloading and she quickly whipped through the video, smiling at the footage that Jack had managed to retrieve, proving who the assassin was. Katarina activated the phone, linking it to the PA system, then gave a thumbs-up.

Nikitin pointed at the door. "Tell him to get ready."

"Yes, sir." Katarina disappeared and Sherrie held up the tablet, its camera activated.

"Control, confirm you're receiving the signal?"

"Confirmed, Skylark, go ahead."

Sherrie gave a thumbs-up to Nikitin. "You're on, sir."

Nikitin squared his shoulders, staring directly into the camera. "For those who don't know who I am, I am Director Ilya Nikitin, head of the FSB. A terrible tragedy has befallen our nation. Our president was assassinated, that fact shared with you yesterday. But I am here to tell you that everything you've heard has been a lie. Go on the Internet now. Check your social media feeds. Newscasters, check your inboxes. The proof of what happened is being transmitted now. The Americans are not responsible for what happened yesterday. Forces loyal to General Kalishnik committed the assassination. The actual assassin's name is Major Aleksie Lukin. We have video footage proving it and we have audio with the assassin and General Kalishnik together, discussing the plot.

"To the Russian troops that are now attacking FSB headquarters, General Kalishnik is not your president. He is a murderer. This is a coup d'état. It's up to you to fight back, otherwise, we lose our nation and we descend into chaos. To the people of Russia, I say, rise up, take to the streets, stop those who would bring us back to the old days. Things aren't perfect, I know, but despite what some would tell you, they are better than they were. Don't let all the hard work from the past thirty years be destroyed because of one man's ambitions.

"As Director of the FSB, I am ordering the immediate arrest of General Kalishnik and Major Lukin, and any of the co-conspirators yet to be named. I am ordering all troops to return to their barracks and await further orders, and I'm calling on everyone to share what we have discovered with your friends, your family, your colleagues. Take to the streets and show it to the men and women in uniform who have sworn an oath to protect this country."

Another shell rocked the building and Sherrie stumbled but regained her balance as Nikitin continued.

"As you can hear, our forces loyal to their country but misinformed, continue to attack. Many of you may ask why you should trust the FSB. I'm not asking you to do any such thing. The FSB isn't your friend. That's not our job. Our job is to protect our country from its enemies. And to do that, we get dirty. But today, our enemies are from within, and I'm calling on you to trust your own eyes, see the evidence for yourselves, and make your own decision. Take to the streets to stop the theft of your country. If you have doubts, stay at home, return to your barracks, and let those you elected to Parliament sort this out."

Another massive explosion rocked the building and the door burst open, Agent Galkin rushing in. "Sir, they're targeting your office. You need to go, now."

Nikitin leaned forward, his knuckles pressed against his desk. "Keep recording," he ordered Sherrie. "My country is more important than my life."

Sherrie stepped closer, centering him in the frame once again.

"My fellow countrymen, I have little time left, and what you do in the coming hours and days will determine the future of Mother Russia for years and decades to come. Stop this madness now before it's too late. Take to the streets. Take back your country. Take back your future."

A massive explosion tore apart the outside wall. Agent Galkin cried out for a brief moment and Katarina screamed from the next room.

And Sherrie blacked out as she was slammed against the inner wall, those sent to silence them finally finding their mark.

Operations Center 3, CIA Headquarters

Langley, Virginia

Leroux leaped to his feet as he activated his comms. The tablet was still transmitting, the image suggesting it was lying on the floor in a pile of rubble, a bloody hand he recognized as Sherrie's, dominating the frame. "Skylark, do you read, over?" No response. "Skylark, Control Actual, do you read, over."

Nothing.

He sank back into his chair. "Skylark, can you make a sound, move your fingers?"

But there was no response as gunfire and howling wind overwhelmed the mic on the tablet. He collapsed forward, his elbows slamming onto the workstation as he clasped his face with his hands, squeezing his eyes shut as he battled the urge to cry out. He had an op to run. He sucked in a breath and forced himself to open his eyes.

He pointed at Packman. "Continue attempting to make contact with her." His voice cracked and the tears flowed, but he didn't bother wiping them away.

"Yes, sir," said Packman, his voice subdued as he fit his headset in place, repeating the call.

Leroux turned to Tong. "Please tell me we got everything recorded."

"Yes, sir. We broadcast it live and now it's being transmitted wide."

He pulled up a dashboard showing the various primary social media sites. The CIA had tens of thousands of fake accounts pushing the story across the globe, sharing and liking the post, driving it up the trending list. The deeper the penetration, the more organic and legitimate interactions that would come into play, and the video along with the evidence associated with it would go viral worldwide.

"What about Russia?"

Tong brought up a separate dashboard. "It's starting to trend. It looks like their censors haven't had a chance to shut it down yet."

Leroux frowned. "They will, eventually. Keep pushing and keep an open channel with the Pentagon. They should be monitoring Russian troop activity. If we start to see units standing down, that could be our first indicator of whether it is working."

"Yes, sir." She had a sympathetic smile, her eyes glistening no doubt over the pain he was feeling more than Sherrie's situation. He turned back to Packman, continuing to call Sherrie to no avail, the image on the screen the same as the gunfire continued.

He closed his eyes again, drawing a calming breath, then Packman exclaimed, "Look!"

Leroux opened his eyes to see figures running past the camera. Men's voices shouted in Russian and the translator in the back of the room, her hands covering her ears as she pressed the headphones harder to hear better. A hand raised into the air, silencing the room. "It sounds like FSB personnel. They're saying, 'Get the director. Someone check on her.'"

The tablet was knocked aside by a boot, changing the angle and Leroux cursed as all they now had was a shot of broken drywall. Excited utterances erupted from the speakers overhead and the translator shot two fists in the air.

"She's alive!"

Server Room S204, The Kremlin

Moscow, Russia

Jack sprayed bursts of 5.45-millimeter rounds at his opponents, mowing several of them down before dropping to a knee and leaning out, switching directions, firing toward the opposite end of the corridor, taking out two more. He quickly did a shoulder check to make sure he was still clear from behind, then reached out and grabbed another assault rifle and as many magazines as he could, tossing them into the server room.

The elevator chimed and shouts erupted. He spun toward the opening doors and took aim. The muzzles of two rifles slowly emerged and he switched to single shot, steadying his breathing. The first soldier emerged but Jack waited for more to reveal themselves. The second stepped out and they made eye contact. Jack squeezed the trigger and the man dropped. Before he hit the floor, Jack had already acquired his next target and opened fire, taking the second down as well.

Panicked debate from within the elevator ensued, though the debate didn't last long. He fired two rounds at the door frame then a boot appeared, kicking the leg of one of the downed men out of the way so the doors could close. He decided they were safe when he heard footsteps behind him.

"It's me," said Teresa.

Jack jerked a thumb over his shoulder at the liberated assault rifle. "Do you know how to use that?"

"Yes."

"Then inspect it and make sure it's not damaged. Our prisoners?"

"I've tied both of them up."

"Our data?"

"Still transmitting, but it doesn't matter." She held out her phone, a video playing. "This is going out everywhere."

Jack took a quick glance to see Director Nikitin delivering an impassioned speech. "What's he saying?" he asked as he retrieved more equipment from the dead soldiers.

"He's calling for the arrest of General Kalishnik and Major Lukin, and calling for troops to return to their barracks and Russians to take to the streets." She stuffed the phone in her pocket but left it playing so they could hear it, and picked up one of the assault rifles, checking it over. "What's our plan?"

Jack shrugged. "Don't really have one. I was sure we'd be dead by now."

"I'm as surprised as you are, but since we are alive, we should look at getting out of here."

"Easier said than done."

"The way I see it, we have two choices. We hole up here as long as we can until cooler heads prevail, or we try to get the hell out of the building, just in case cooler heads don't prevail."

"Holing up is a risky option."

Teresa tapped her pocket, still playing the video. "This has to work, doesn't it?"

Jack pursed his lips. "It has to. But will it?"

The elevator doors chimed again, narrowing their options to one. He took aim and jerked his chin over his shoulder at the far end of the corridor. "Watch our six. There's a stairwell at the far end. They might try to come in while we're distracted."

"I've got you covered." She reached out and removed the body armor from one of the downed soldiers. "Jack, put this on."

He quickly fit it in place as the elevator doors opened, smoke canisters rolling out, rapidly filling the corridor with a thick fog, eerie billowing shadows cast by the emergency lighting that stretched from one end to the other. He dropped, prone on the floor, then took a bead on where the elevator should be, firing a single shot before shifting ten degrees and shooting again. He rapidly repeated the process and someone shouted out in agony as one of his rounds found its mark, then another. Gunfire erupted from the enemy position, bullets spraying over their heads as Teresa lay beside him, using one of the dead soldiers as cover as she watched the far end of the corridor.

"Here they come," she said. "They've popped smoke."

Jack didn't bother looking. He trusted Teresa to cover them as he continued to pump single rounds into the smoke each time he spotted a muzzle flash. Teresa's phone continued to play Nikitin's speech on a loop, and it gave him an idea. "Turn your phone up to max and give it to me."

She pulled it out and the volume got louder before it was placed in his hand.

"You need to listen to this!" he shouted in Russian, then whipped the phone along the floor toward the elevators like it was shuffleboard night at the seniors' center. More shots rang out in response, but the phone continued to play.

"Stop shooting and listen!" he shouted as gunfire from the far end rang out.

"Do I respond?" asked Teresa.

"Stand by. Right now, they can't see us. They have just as much chance of hitting their own people as they do us." He raised his voice. "Listen to the recording! That's Director Nikitin of the FSB. He's calling for the arrest of General Kalishnik. They have proof that he's behind the assassination. You have to listen to what is being said."

The gunfire from the elevator position waned and he continued to hold fire, the only shots now from the far end of the corridor.

"Fall back!" shouted someone from within the smoke near the elevator. Jack held his fire then heard the doors of the elevator shut, the only sounds now coming from the stairwell and Teresa's phone.

"What do we do now?"

Jack repositioned to support Teresa. "Let's force them back. Hopefully, their friends will talk to them."

"Do you really think they're going to let us go?"

"Hell no. My guess is they've fallen back to find out what's going on. But even if they stand down, we still killed a bunch of their buddies. They're not going to forgive us for that." He squeezed off several rounds toward the far end, as did Teresa. A barrage of gunfire replied. "Switch to full auto."

"Done."

"You sweep left to right, I'll take right to left, chest height. Open fire." Both AK-74 assault rifles belched lead toward the far end of the corridor, their targets, hidden in the smoke, crying out as the bullets found their marks.

"Hold your fire!"

Both weapons fell silent and the Russians responded as the sounds of moaning men and bodies dragging on tile cut through the smoke before the strained hiss of a pneumatic door spring doing its job fell silent, the door to the stairwell clicking shut, leaving them alone.

For the moment.

"What now?"

"Now it's time to take the fight to them."

FSB Headquarters

Moscow, Russia

Sherrie jerked her head away from the pungent odor, her eyes fluttering open.

"Are you all right?" asked a concerned voice in Russian.

It took her a moment to figure out just where the hell she was. She sucked in a deep breath, her entire body aching with the effort.

"Are you all right?"

She shook her head, regretting it, then pushed away the smelling salts about to be employed once again. "I don't know."

She wiggled her fingers and bent her arms at the elbow, then rotated her shoulders and gently twisted her neck. Every move hurt, but nothing seemed broken. She repeated the process with her legs and gave a nod. "I think I'll live." She gasped. "Director Nikitin, is he all right?"

"I've seen better days," came a voice from her right. She turned to see the man sitting in a chair, his face cut and bleeding in several places.

"You look terrible, sir."

Nikitin grunted. "Find that woman a mirror."

The man tending to her gave her a sympathetic smile. "Sorry, miss, you look like shit as well."

She laughed. "Oh well, they always say, the looks are the first to go. What's our status?"

Nikitin waved a hand, leaving the report to one of his underlings.

"The enemy has breached the outer walls. It's not safe to return fire from the windows. They have attack helicopters now, strafing the buildings. We've managed to hold them to the courtyard, but several of the minor buildings have been breached. It's only a matter of time before they're inside this building and then it'll be a floor-to-floor fight, but at least their heavy weapons will be taken out of the equation."

"And the speech?"

"It's spreading, but so far no effect, or at least none that we're aware of. Our ability to communicate with the outside world is gone. The cellular networks are jammed and all hard lines are cut. Our satellite array was taken out by the helicopters."

"My tablet, do you have it?"

"No."

"I need to get it. If it's still operational, we should be able to communicate with the outside world."

"How?"

She smirked. "If I told you, I'd have to kill you."

The man laughed and extended a hand, helping her to her feet. "Where'd you last have it?"

"In the director's office."

The man shook his head. "You don't want to go in there. It's not safe."

"I have no choice."

Two men rushed in, addressing Nikitin. "Sir, he's ready to see you now."

Nikitin rose, reaching out for the wall, his balance unsteady. Everyone in the room, including Sherrie, rushed to lend him a hand but he waved them off, instead steadying himself then brushing off his suit jacket. "I'm all right. Let's go."

The door opened and from Sherrie's new position she could see what lay on the other side.

And her jaw dropped at who was standing there. "What the hell's going on?"

Sublevel 2, The Kremlin

Moscow, Russia

Jack forced the doors of the elevator open then shot the shit out of the cables, the elevator car overhead dropping before the emergency brakes kicked in, bringing the car to a screeching halt, but also disabling this method of access to their level for some time. He closed the outer doors, then double-checked both ends of the corridor, the smoke still thick with the power to the ventilation system shut down. They had stacked bodies three high to act as sandbagged emplacements, giving them protection from either end of the corridor, with body armor draped strategically to provide additional protection, all their weapons and ammo gathered inside their small position.

He picked up her phone, still playing whatever feed she had accessed, and slid it down the floor, back toward her as his comms chirped in his ear. He breathed a sigh of relief at Leroux's voice.

"Jackrabbit, Control Actual. Do you read, over?"

"I read you, Control."

"It's about damn time. We just reestablished comms. The signal's weak," explained Leroux. "There must be some sort of jamming going on where you are."

The signal was digital, static replaced with clipping, and as Jack returned to their fortified position, it got worse.

"Signal strength is dropping, Jackrabbit."

Jack cursed, returning to the elevator shaft. "How's that?"

"Much better."

"Looks like I can only get a good signal near the elevator shaft, which is not a good place to be. If I have to return to our fortified position at the server room, we'll probably lose contact."

"Understood. Sitrep?"

"The battery backup is dead, so you won't be receiving any more data from us. We've managed to hold them off for now and we played some of the audio from Nikitin's speech for them that had them backing off, probably to figure out what the hell's going on. I'm not confident though that they won't return in force with the proper equipment to overwhelm us. Once they come in with grenades and ballistic shields, we're screwed. Sitrep on your end?"

"Russian forces have penetrated FSB headquarters. It looks like both sides are taking heavy casualties, with the army winning due to superior firepower."

"Sherrie?"

"Wounded but alive, as is Director Nikitin. We've lost communications for the moment, but we're attempting to reestablish them."

"And the broadcast?"

"Number one trending topic on all major social media platforms. Every major news network outside of Russia is carrying it, including China."

"That's nice but doesn't help us. What the hell's happening inside Russia?"

"None of the state-controlled media are covering it, of course. The pirate networks are but the Russians have just started scrubbing it."

"Where's General Kalishnik?"

"As far as we know, he's still at the Kremlin. His office has given notice that he'll be making an address to the nation in about fifteen minutes."

"You know anything he says is going to be a lie."

"Of course."

"And a lot of people are going to believe those lies."

"You're not suggesting what I think you're suggesting?"

"I don't think we have a choice."

Leroux cursed. "I'm going to have to clear it. An American asset assassinating a Russian president is what got this whole thing started."

"Get it cleared and get me a way in. One way or another, General Kalishnik cannot be allowed to give that speech."

Director Nikitin's Office, FSB Headquarters

Moscow, Russia

Sherrie didn't bother searching the rubble for her comms knocked out of her ear canal from the force of the explosion. It was too tiny. She quickly found the tablet, however, the glow of its screen revealing its position near the inner wall, the entire outer wall and windows now gone. She grabbed the tablet and rushed back to the outer office, frowning at the sight of the secretary's body lying on the floor, her face covered by a jacket.

Sherrie stepped into the corridor and was escorted to the room where Nikitin was now meeting with a man who shouldn't and couldn't be there, but that wasn't her concern at the moment. None of it would matter if they couldn't get the message out. The screen was cracked but it was still functioning. The question was whether the camera was still working. She flipped it around. "I don't know if you guys are getting this, but I've lost comms. Can you signal the tablet?"

She flipped it back around and the tablet pinged with a message. She tapped on it.

We're reading you. Good to hear your voice.

She gently ran her hand over the screen, picturing the love of her life and what he must have gone through when the room was taken out. She flipped the tablet around again. "Make sure you're recording this and get ready to transmit it live. You're not going to believe who's here. No time to explain."

The tablet pinged with an acknowledgment as she was led into the room. Nikitin smiled at her and held out a hand, inviting her over.

"Sir, I'd like you to meet a very brave woman who's been instrumental in getting out the truth."

The diminutive man extended a hand and she shook it, her skin crawling at the touch of evil, though today, he was the lesser of two.

Operations Center 3, CIA Headquarters

Langley, Virginia

Morrison rushed into the room, Leroux having sent him a message indicating a new broadcast was about to come through. Director McQuay was on his heels and they joined him at the center of the room. Sherrie's tablet was still transmitting, but her hand holding it was resting by her side, giving them a gently swaying view of the wall of a room as voices talked in Russian.

Morrison held up a finger as he cocked an ear. "Wait a minute, General Kalishnik is there?"

"That's what it sounds like, sir. According to the translator, they keep referring to another man in the room as Mr. President."

"But I thought he was about to give a speech at the Kremlin? And why the hell would he be there, glad-handing with Nikitin, his archrival?"

"I have no idea, sir."

The translator rose. "That's not General Kalishnik. The voice isn't deep enough, it's not gravelly enough."

Leroux snapped his fingers at Tong. "Isolate his voice, see if we can match it."

"On it."

Tong worked her station as the camera suddenly swung, two men centered in the frame, Director Nikitin on the left, and on the right, someone who looked remarkably good for a dead man, the assassinated Russian president.

"What the hell is going on?" exclaimed Morrison. "He's supposed to be dead! My God, the entire world is about to go to war because it thinks he's dead! What the hell is he doing alive?"

Director McQuay was already on her phone, no doubt to the White House, as an impossible speech commenced.

FSB Headquarters

Moscow, Russia

"Citizens of Russia, friends, I stand before you very much alive. The deception of the past twenty-four hours was necessary, but thanks to the heroic efforts of the FSB, we now know the truth. Less than one week ago, Director Nikitin approached me, indicating there was evidence an attempt was to be made on my life by a faction within the command structure that wasn't happy with the direction Russia has been heading. Several of those suspected of being involved suddenly went to Warsaw two days ago, and during this illegal operation, these traitors kidnapped an American Embassy worker, a face you've all seen on television, a man known as Jack Palance.

"I'm here to tell you he's innocent and has nothing to do with the attempt on my life. Thanks to the brilliant investigative skills of our friends at the FSB, they were able to determine who the perpetrators were, and then identify who was behind this. By now, you've heard the audio recording of General Kalishnik speaking to the assassin, Major Lukin. I'm here to tell you that that recording is genuine. Any statement to the contrary is a lie.

"The video you saw of my assassination is genuine, though cleverly manipulated to make it appear as if America were behind it. The final frames were faked, but the cold-blooded murder depicted was real. When Director Nikitin informed me that the assassination plot had been triggered, under his recommendation, one of my doubles was substituted, and I have been safely staying here at FSB Headquarters while the truth was determined.

"Now that it has been, I am reasserting my powers as president of our great nation. I call upon all troops now surrounding FSB Headquarters to stand down and return to barracks. I am calling for the arrest of General Kalishnik, Major Lukin, and anyone else involved in the plot to overthrow the legitimate leader of this great nation. And I call on the citizens to rise up and take to the streets. This is *your* country, not General Kalishnik's."

The building shook with another massive explosion, word obviously not having reached the tank gunners. The president remained on his feet, his eyes staring into the camera that Sherrie gripped.

"Citizens of Russia, it's time to end this. It's time to take back our country from those who crave war, before it's too late." He made a gesture with his hand below the frame and Sherrie tapped the button to stop the recording. She checked the status of the file and it indicated it had streamed successfully.

"Did you get that?" she asked Leroux, her voice low.

A message arrived a moment later.

We got it and it's been going out live. We're putting it on a loop and adding it to all the feeds.

"Acknowledged." She held up the tablet and addressed the president. "Mr. President, I've confirmed that your broadcast went out live and is now being distributed to every news organization and device possible."

He acknowledged her statement then turned to Nikitin. "When this is all said and done, no mention can be made that it was the Americans that saved us."

"Of course not," said Nikitin, giving Sherrie a look.

Sherrie bowed slightly. "While I can't speak for Washington, I'm quite certain avoiding war is their ultimate goal, not who gets the credit."

Another shell shook the building as a helicopter blasted past, its cannons opening up on one of the lower floors.

The tablet pinged with another message.

Four Sukhoi fighters inbound on your position. Seek shelter!

Sherrie cursed and stepped toward the two men she never thought she would be cheering for just one day ago. "Sirs, we have reports of four Sukhois inbound. We need to get to a bomb shelter immediately."

Nikitin snapped his fingers and one of the FSB agents got on his radio as four more rushed into the room, guiding everyone toward a stairwell at the end of the corridor.

Perhaps telling the world where you were hiding wasn't such a wise move.

Operations Center 3, CIA Headquarters

Langley, Virginia

"TASS is broadcasting the president's speech!" announced an excited Packman as he brought up the feed.

Leroux was about to ask which president when the news report cut to what had just been recorded. Text scrolled below the speech and he pointed at it. "What's the scroll say?"

Morrison translated. "It's saying that the authenticity of the recording hasn't been confirmed, however, it's believed to be genuine."

"There's something you need to see," said Tong as she tapped the keyboard and brought up satellite footage of FSB Headquarters.

"What are we looking at?" asked Morrison as Leroux eyed the display, showing hundreds if not thousands of people swarming toward the buildings under assault.

"Are those reinforcements?" asked Child.

"No. Look." Tong zoomed in. It was dark now, but the computer-enhanced image clearly showed the new arrivals were unarmed civilians.

They surrounded the soldiers, holding up their phones, and soon the muzzle flashes slowly subsided.

"I've got footage from the ground," said Packman. "People are live streaming."

"Put some of it up," instructed Leroux.

Moments later, half a dozen different feeds from cellphone cameras appeared, showing people young and old hugging each other and celebrating as each soldier lowered his weapon. Leroux's eyes narrowed as he spotted something. "Give us the audio on number three."

The speakers overhead came alive with song, and Leroux smiled at the sound of thousands singing the Russian national anthem, the gunfire rapidly fading away. "Status on those inbounds?" He glanced over at the map showing the four targets rapidly closing in on FSB Headquarters.

"No change," reported Tong. "They're still inbound."

Leroux cursed and sat at his terminal, sending a message to Sherrie.

What's your status?

She replied over the speakers. "Control, we're in the stairwell heading to the bomb shelter. ETA on those inbounds?"

Tong held up two fingers and Leroux relayed the info.

2 minutes.

"What are we going to do?" asked Child. "They're probably carrying enough firepower to level the entire complex."

Director McQuay frowned. "They're following their orders. They have no idea what's happening on the ground."

Morrison agreed. "Unless they receive authenticated orders countermanding their mission, there's no stopping them."

Leroux typed furiously.

You've got to hurry. They could launch at any moment.

Jack's voice cut in. "Control, Jackrabbit, we're in position. Are we a go, over?"

Leroux turned to Morrison who then faced the director. "Are we a go?"

She nodded. "Do it, and let's just pray we aren't about to make things worse."

Approaching the Press Room, The Kremlin

Moscow, Russia

Jack was filthy, yet Teresa appeared remarkably none the worse for wear. He was convinced it was because he was in the lead, acting as a broom in the filthy air ducts they had crawled through. They had used the disabled elevator shaft to gain access to the main level, then a series of air shafts that now had him peering out a vent and into the press room where they were set up for General Kalishnik's address to the nation. The room was filled with reporters and security, everyone excitedly staring at their phones, as stunned as he was at the revelation their late president wasn't so late after all.

Teresa tapped his foot and he glanced back at her. "What?" he whispered.

"Let me take the shot."

He shook his head. "This is no time to prove yourself."

"You don't understand. A Russian has to take that shot. It can't be an American. It must be a Russian."

He frowned. She was right. It would be better if a Russian took the shot. It was actually ironic that here he was about to shoot a Russian president under orders from Washington to do so, the exact scenario he was framed for twenty-four hours earlier. The problem was that they couldn't afford to miss. "Are you a good shot?"

"Good enough."

Unfortunately, "good enough" wasn't good enough an answer. "Sorry, we can't risk you missing, but you're right, a Russian needs to take the shot."

"Jack—"

He cut her off. "Here's what we'll do. I'll take the shot. As soon as I confirm the kill, I hand you the gun. You've got gunpowder residue all over you from the firefight earlier. They'll believe you did it."

She frowned. "You're right. We've only got one shot at this."

He grunted. "Literally."

The room on the other side of the vent erupted in excitement, shouting questions at the imposter president as he emerged from a side entrance. The man stepped up to the podium and held up a hand, silencing the crowd gathered.

"I'm here to address the recent broadcast you have all no doubt seen by now. I have only one thing to say. Fake news! We've already determined that these recordings are being pushed from American servers and I can assure you they are lies."

"Are you saying the president's speech from a few minutes ago is fake?" shouted one of the reporters.

"I'm the president. That man is an imposter."

Jack loosened the final screw holding the grate in place with his Swiss Army knife. "Ready?"

Teresa tapped his foot. "Ready."

He brought his weapon forward then took a breath, steadying his nerves as Kalishnik droned on, continually challenged by the skeptical press. Jack's left hand darted out, punching the grill out of the way, then his right arm extended out and he took a bead on Kalishnik as a guard shouted nearby.

"Mr. President, look out!"

Jack squeezed the trigger twice, both rounds slamming into Kalishnik's chest. He fired a third round when he didn't see blood, fearing the man might be wearing a vest. The third shot found its mark, blasting a hole in the man's forehead. Screams erupted as did gunfire. Teresa yanked on his legs, pulling him back as the guards responded. They scrambled backward to a junction that allowed them to turn around. They exchanged weapons and he winked at her. "Who knew you were a crack shot?"

She grinned. "You know I can never take my weapons proficiency exam ever again if we're to make them believe I did this."

Jack chuckled. "This is true." They continued their escape and came to another junction. "I think this is as good a place as any to hole up."

She shrugged. "I suppose so."

Jack sighed and lay on his side as Teresa did the same in the opposite direction. He propped his head up and stared into her eyes. "I can think of a few ways we can kill the time."

"Eww."

His head jerked back in mock affront. "What do you mean, eww?"

"I mean, you're still wearing Lieutenant Colonel Aminoff's face. He is not an attractive man."

Jack laughed. "Are you really that shallow that it's all about looks for you?"

"I'm sure if I got to know the man and he turned out to be sweet, I could be attracted to him, but right here, right now, in the heat of the moment, well, let's just say there's no heat."

Jack sighed. "Oh, well, I guess I'm not going out with a bang."

Bomb Shelter, FSB Headquarters

Moscow, Russia

Sherrie took a knee in the bomb shelter, something left over from the Cold War. It was deep enough and impressive enough that she was certain they would survive the inbound conventional attack. The president sat at a conference room table with Nikitin and several other senior advisors, while anyone else who had managed to make it to the room before the massive metal door shut the moment the president cleared, sat around the perimeter. What was sad was that the shelter was far more than just a conference room, but once those doors had shut, everyone outside was cut off, though she supposed there probably wasn't enough time for most of those still alive to seek cover.

Her tablet's connection with Langley had cut off the moment the doors shut, and her heart ached as she imagined what her love must be going through. He would witness the destruction, he would witness the aftermath, and he would assume she was dead until they could be finally dug out, if they ever were. If General Kalishnik remained in power long enough, it wouldn't matter if the real president were still alive.

"I have external communications," announced one of the FSB staff manning a bank of computers at the far end of the room. "Mr. President, you have to hear this!"

"What is it?"

"General Kalishnik! He's been assassinated, live on television!" The man pressed a headset tighter against his ear. "Somebody shot him at the beginning of the press conference, two to the chest, one to the head."

Cheers erupted in the room and the president exchanged a handshake and smile with Nikitin.

"Can we confirm this?" asked Nikitin.

"I'm trying to pull up video now…I've got it." The staffer pressed a button then turned toward a large screen on the wall. Everyone in the room faced it, and Sherrie smiled as the bastard shook from each round before dropping like a sack of potatoes from a shot so good, she had a feeling Jack was responsible, though she kept that opinion to herself. Handshakes, back slaps, and fist bumps rounded the room as Sherrie checked her watch. Two minutes had passed. In fact, several more.

She cleared her throat. "Shouldn't we have been hit by now?"

Nikitin checked his own watch. "It's certainly been more than two minutes. I think we need to risk cracking the door."

The president nodded. "Agreed."

Nikitin instructed one of the men to open the outer door and Sherrie followed. The moment it was opened, she should have comms back. The FSB agent instructed the guards manning the door to open it. They exchanged nervous glances, but complied, unlocking then easily pushing aside the perfectly balanced door.

She activated her camera. "Control, Skylark. Do you read, over?"

A message arrived a moment later.

We read you, Skylark. What's your status?

"Alive and kicking. Report."

The reply took some time to come through, and she wondered if she had lost the connection again. Her tablet pinged.

General Kalishnik is dead. Jack took him out a few minutes ago. Less than thirty seconds after that, the inbound fighters bugged out and are now returning to base. The attack on your position has been stopped. Thousands of civilians are on the streets surrounding the troops that were attacking. The troop carriers are just starting to load up now. It looks like they're returning to barracks and the helicopters that were strafing you have left. It looks like it's over.

Her shoulders slumped in relief. "And Jack?"

He's holed up in the ductwork with Teresa, waiting for the all-clear. Right now, the Kremlin's a mess. No one knows who's in charge.

"Understood. I'll see what I can do about that from this end. Skylark, out."

Everyone around the door was staring at her, desperate for news, and she smiled. "The air strike's been called off. The troops outside have stood down and are returning to barracks. We're safe."

One of the guards grabbed her in a bear hug, lifting her off her feet, and she laughed. "Put me down. I have to tell the president."

The man did as told, and as the celebration continued, she hurried back to the conference room. All eyes were on her.

"Report," snapped Nikitin.

She bowed slightly. "Sir, Mr. President, I'm pleased to inform you that the airstrike has been called off. The helicopters have departed and the troops outside are preparing to return to barracks. General Kalishnik is indeed dead, but apparently there's confusion at the Kremlin. I highly recommend we get there as quickly as possible to reestablish order."

The president rose. "She's right. It's time to take back my country."

The Kremlin

Moscow, Russia

It had been forty-five boring minutes. The shagadelic good time he had offered Teresa certainly would have killed the minutes a lot faster than their whispered conversation, but he had kissed in these masks before and it wasn't very pleasant. It just didn't feel natural. No matter how real a face might look, there was nothing like the touch of real skin on skin. The first twenty minutes after the assassination had been filled with panic and confusion. They could hear the shouts coming through the air ducts, punctuated by bursts of gunfire, but there hadn't been shots for at least ten minutes now, and the yelling had stopped.

Langley was providing periodic updates, the chaos from the press conference still broadcasting live, nobody cutting the feed. Apparently, Kalishnik's body had been carried out as guards cleared the room, but oddly, no one had pursued his killers beyond the initial barrage of gunfire. He supposed it made sense. The common soldier who had declared their loyalty to Kalishnik had done so because they believed he was the legitimately chosen successor, since both the upper and lower houses of the legislature had named him as such. But with the real president alive, and the evidence now out there about what had actually happened, he was certain those in uniform were questioning their orders and weren't eager to get involved in a shootout with someone who might have just killed a traitor.

"Jackrabbit, Control, come in, over."

Jack activated his comms. "This is Jackrabbit. Go ahead, Control."

"Good news. You can come out now."

He cocked an eyebrow. "Are you sure?"

"Yes. The president has arrived along with Nikitin. He's about to address the Duma in a speech that's going out live worldwide. Sherrie and a contingent of FSB personnel are waiting for you in the press briefing room where you took the shots. You can come out there."

"Understood. Tell her we'll be there in a few minutes."

"Will do. Control, out."

Jack gave Teresa a kiss.

"Eww."

He laughed. "We'll be out of these soon. The president is here. It's over. Sherrie is waiting for us in the press room." He scurried backward and Teresa followed, then he turned himself around at a junction, and minutes later, they were approaching the gaping hole where he had ended things.

"Friendlies approaching!" he called.

Sherrie replied. "Acknowledged. You're clear."

Jack scrambled forward then tentatively poked his head through the hole to find Sherrie smiling at him, plus a dozen guards covering her, their bodies all turned away, protecting them from anyone who might enter the room.

"Fancy meeting you here," he said as he scrambled out and onto the floor.

"I was told you were tired of playing mouse in the house," said Sherrie as Jack helped Teresa down. "That was one hell of a shot."

Jack slapped Teresa on the shoulder. "Who knew she could shoot the balls off a gnat?"

Sherrie's micro-reaction in her eyes indicated she was surprised at who had taken the shot, but she didn't give away the secret. "Congratulations. Now, if you'll follow me, I have a car waiting outside."

"Lead the way."

The contingent wound through the corridors, the floors and walls stained with blood from where those caught up in the chaos had paid the ultimate price. They were soon outside in another crisp, Moscow winter night. They climbed into a waiting SUV, the driver pulling away the moment the last door slammed shut. He glanced over at Jack, sitting in the passenger seat.

"Don't worry, you can speak freely. I'm from the embassy. We've been assured safe passage by the Russian president. I'm taking you to the embassy, then you'll be heading directly for the airport. You'll be stateside by tomorrow."

"Does that include me?" asked Teresa.

"It does," confirmed Sherrie.

Jack reached back and took Teresa's hand, giving it a squeeze. "See, I told you it would all work out."

"Did you?"

He shrugged. "I must have. I'm a very positive guy." He turned on the radio. "Let's see if we can catch some of the president's speech."

Their driver took over the controls, selecting one of the local news-talk stations, and Jack cursed at the first words they heard.

"But one thing is clear. We must be firmer in our resolve. Russia must be stronger than ever before. And to that end, we will redouble our efforts, strengthening our military capabilities, increasing our internal security, so we make certain the tragic events of the past twenty-four hours never happen again. We will redouble our efforts in Ukraine and emerge from this crisis victorious—"

Jack reached forward and turned off the radio. "Welcome to the new Russia, same as the old."

Waldorf Astoria

Washington, D.C.

Jack lay in the king-size bed, staring into Teresa's eyes. It had been a week since the events that had brought them together, and the world was back to normal. The Russian president was once again in control and had cleaned house, anyone in the command structure that had declared loyalty to General Kalishnik was gone. Kalishnik's body was paraded on TV, then hours later, so was Major Lukin's, his corpse found among a cluster of loyalists killed in the minutes following the general's assassination. Russian, American, NATO, and Chinese forces had all stood down to normal readiness levels, with America once again at DEFCON 5.

The world had avoided a disaster.

Or perhaps had merely postponed it.

"I think I'm going to like America."

He smiled at her. "You will, but after today, we'll never see each other again."

She sighed. "That's too bad. But what's that American saying, never say never?"

He chuckled as he ran his fingers through her hair. "I suppose that's true. Anything's possible."

"It's too bad that nothing's changed after everything that's happened."

Jack agreed. "Unfortunately, I think things have changed. If anything, he's become more hardline. That should placate his opponents for now, but should he win in Ukraine, I'd hate to see what comes next. But one thing's for sure, democracy is truly dead in Russia."

"Yes, but at least General Kalishnik failed in his attempt to recreate the Soviet Union. You heard what they found gripped in his hand when they examined the body?"

Jack nodded. "Yes, a Soviet-era pin. Apparently, he carried it with him everywhere, a constant reminder of the past where in his mind things were better. He was a man who had no interest in the lessons history can teach us."

His phone vibrated and he rolled over, grabbing it off the nightstand to see a message.

Thank you! Thank you! Thank you!

He laughed and replied with a thumbs-up.

"Who was that?"

He rolled back over and took Teresa in his arms. "That was Sherrie, thanking me for sending her boyfriend a copy of the Operations Officer Intimate Encounters Handbook."

Teresa smiled. "I've read that book. There's something on page thirty-seven I've always wanted to try."

Jack tossed the sheets over their heads. "I think I know what you're talking about." He maneuvered into position and she squealed.

"That's the one!"

THE END

ACKNOWLEDGMENTS

This book was a lot of fun to write. Ever since I created the character of Jack in The Tomb of Genghis Khan, I've wanted to get to know him better. I've teased him out over several novels, and decided it was time to really get to know him.

This is the first in a planned series, and I think it will be a lot of fun to write. It's always a joy to be laughing when you're writing, and I can only imagine what my transcribers are thinking when they read some of the craziness I dictate.

Now, here's a funny little tidbit. The joke about Marc Therrien's Christmas Day schedule? That's real, and was taken from my past where I had a manager who actually accidentally shared that EXACT same calendar. It was discovered and widely shared. He wasn't well-liked.

Oh, and if history from so far back is to be believed, Sun Tzu never lost a battle. Though there is a lot of debate.

As usual, there are people to thank. Brent Richards for some weapons info, Isabelle Laprise-Enright for some female undergarment help, my dad for all the research, and, as always, my wife, daughter, my late mother who will always be an angel on my shoulder as I write, as well as my friends for their continued support, and my fantastic proofreading team!

To those who have not already done so, please visit my website at www.jrobertkennedy.com, then sign up for the Insider's Club to be notified of new book releases. Your email address will never be shared or sold.

Thank you once again for reading.